# Charmed

# Also From Lexi Blake

ROMANTIC SUSPENSE

**Masters and Mercenaries**
The Dom Who Loved Me
The Men With The Golden Cuffs
A Dom is Forever
On Her Master's Secret Service
Sanctum: A Masters and Mercenaries Novella
Love and Let Die
Unconditional: A Masters and Mercenaries Novella
Dungeon Royale
Dungeon Games: A Masters and Mercenaries Novella
A View to a Thrill
Cherished: A Masters and Mercenaries Novella
You Only Love Twice
Luscious: Masters and Mercenaries~Topped
Adored: A Masters and Mercenaries Novella
Master No
Just One Taste: Masters and Mercenaries~Topped 2
From Sanctum with Love
Devoted: A Masters and Mercenaries Novella
Dominance Never Dies
Submission is Not Enough
Master Bits and Mercenary Bites~The Secret Recipes of Topped
Perfectly Paired: Masters and Mercenaries~Topped 3
For His Eyes Only
Arranged: A Masters and Mercenaries Novella
Love Another Day
At Your Service: Masters and Mercenaries~Topped 4
Master Bits and Mercenary Bites~Girls Night
Nobody Does It Better
Close Cover
Protected: A Masters and Mercenaries Novella
Enchanted: A Masters and Mercenaries Novella
Charmed: A Masters and Mercenaries Novella

URBAN FANTASY

**Thieves**
Steal the Light
Steal the Day
Steal the Moon
Steal the Sun
Steal the Night
Ripper
Addict
Sleeper
Outcast
Stealing Summer, Coming soon!

LEXI BLAKE WRITING AS SOPHIE OAK

**Texas Sirens**
Small Town Siren
Siren in the City
Siren Enslaved
Siren Beloved
Siren in Waiting
Siren in Bloom
Siren Unleashed
Siren Reborn

**Nights in Bliss, Colorado**
Three to Ride
Two to Love
One to Keep
Lost in Bliss
Found in Bliss
Pure Bliss
Chasing Bliss
Once Upon a Time in Bliss
Back in Bliss
Sirens in Bliss

**A Faery Story**
Bound
Beast
Beauty

**Standalone**
Away From Me
Snowed In

# Charmed
## A Masters and Mercenaries Novella
# By Lexi Blake

1001 DARK NIGHTS
PRESS

Charmed
A Masters and Mercenaries Novella
By Lexi Blake

1001 Dark Nights

Published by 1001 Dark Nights Press, an imprint of Evil Eye Concepts, Incorporated

# Acknowledgments from the Author

Thanks to everyone who helped make Charmed a reality! JT is a character who's been in my head since long before the first Masters and Mercenaries book was published. Thanks to Kim Guidroz who read the original JT Malone all those years ago.

As always thanks to my team – Kim, Rich, Maria, Jillian, Stormy, Riane, Kori, and Sara. Special thanks to the amazing women of Evil Eye and 1001 Dark Nights – Liz Berry, MJ Rose, and Jillian Stein. You ladies move mountains.

Sign up for the 1001 Dark Nights Newsletter
and be entered to win a Tiffany Key necklace.

There's a contest every month!

Go to www.1001DarkNights.com to subscribe.

**As a bonus, all subscribers can download
FIVE FREE exclusive books!**

# One Thousand and One Dark Nights

*Once upon a time, in the future…*

*I was a student fascinated with stories and learning.
I studied philosophy, poetry, history, the occult, and
the art and science of love and magic. I had a vast
library at my father's home and collected thousands
of volumes of fantastic tales.*

*I learned all about ancient races and bygone
times. About myths and legends and dreams of all
people through the millennium. And the more I read
the stronger my imagination grew until I discovered
that I was able to travel into the stories... to actually
become part of them.*

*I wish I could say that I listened to my teacher
and respected my gift, as I ought to have. If I had, I
would not be telling you this tale now.
But I was foolhardy and confused, showing off
with bravery.*

*One afternoon, curious about the myth of the
Arabian Nights, I traveled back to ancient Persia to
see for myself if it was true that every day Shahryar
(Persian: شهریار, "king") married a new virgin, and then
sent yesterday's wife to be beheaded. It was written
and I had read that by the time he met Scheherazade,
the vizier's daughter, he'd killed one thousand
women.*

*Something went wrong with my efforts. I arrived in the midst of the story and somehow exchanged places with Scheherazade – a phenomena that had never occurred before and that still to this day, I cannot explain.*

*Now I am trapped in that ancient past. I have taken on Scheherazade's life and the only way I can protect myself and stay alive is to do what she did to protect herself and stay alive.*

*Every night the King calls for me and listens as I spin tales. And when the evening ends and dawn breaks, I stop at a point that leaves him breathless and yearning for more. And so the King spares my life for one more day, so that he might hear the rest of my dark tale.*

*As soon as I finish a story... I begin a new one... like the one that you, dear reader, have before you now.*

# Chapter One

*Dallas, TX*

"You need to get laid."

Nina Blunt bit back a groan at the words and held her hand up to indicate to the bartender that she was definitely going to need another glass of wine. She adored Sandra Croft, the woman sitting beside her at the bar, but sometimes she could be a lot to take. She'd met Sandra months before when she'd shown up at the London office of McKay-Taggart and Knight with her daughter and granddaughter. Like many people Nina knew, Sandra was ex-military, and it showed in her no-nonsense, take-no-prisoners style of conversation.

"I'm not here to get laid. I'm here to do a job, and that job starts tomorrow afternoon," Nina pointed out, sliding her empty wine glass forward so the bartender could pour out some more Pinot Noir.

Sandra turned in her chair, her hand on the beer she'd ordered. "When was the last time you got laid? I'm thinking it's been a couple of years. Fess up. I've got a bet on this."

This rarely happened in London. There was a reason she didn't come work for the Dallas team often. Ever, really. It was her first time working directly with Ian Taggart's team, and this was what she got. "It's absolutely none of your business."

"I totally disagree. I have to go undercover with you. I'm your backup. I need to make sure my girl is loose and ready to rumble. I've got some thoughts on hookers."

Sometimes with Sandra she just had to go with it. Often with Sandra, things got so over-the-top awkward it was amusing. "I think they're called gigolos when they're male."

Sandra shook her head. "I refuse that terminology. Look, a doctor's a doctor whether said doc has lady bits or dangly parts or anything in between. A pro's a pro. If there's one thing my daughter's generation has right, it's sexual fluidity."

Sometimes it was utterly fascinating to watch Sandra go. It was one of the reasons she was kind of excited about the upcoming job. Sure, it was a fairly simple catch-the-corporate-spy-in-action job that she'd done a hundred times, but Sandra was her backup and that meant the world might explode. "So you think I should call up an agency and tell them I'll take whatever they send. Girl parts. Boy parts. Doesn't matter."

"I'm only saying these people are professionals and strap-ons exist."

The bartender nearly dropped the bottle of wine she'd been pouring. That happened a lot around Sandra. The woman had no filter and absolutely no fucks to give. Still, she had to smile. Many good things had come out of the mission that had finally brought the Lost Boys full circle, but meeting Sandra had been a blessing to Nina. Sandra had become her friend, and she needed a friend who took no bullshit and told no lies. It was refreshing, even if sometimes challenging. "Well, I will certainly keep that in mind if I feel like I need a good snog."

"You need more than a snog," Sandra pointed out. "Your shoulders are up around your ears. You know they're not supposed to be there, right?"

She couldn't help it if she was a bit on the Type A side of the personality scale. It had served her well in her profession. Well, mostly. "What do you think the wine is for?"

Sandra considered her for a moment. "I think you'll have two glasses of wine, and even though you might want a third, you'll refuse. Like at dinner. You wanted dessert but turned it away. You'll drink the amount of wine you've agreed you can have and then you'll be in bed by nine alone. You'll read a romance novel but when ten o'clock strikes, no matter how much you want to read more, you'll close the book and turn out the lights because you have a schedule."

Well, put like that her evening sounded boring. Yes, she'd wanted the cheeseburger and settled for the grilled chicken salad sans dressing. Yes, she'd wanted a taste of chocolate cake, but a taste tended to lead to eating the whole thing, and then she might gain a pound and he would…

She wasn't really thinking of Roger, was she? She wasn't still making choices based on the humiliation he might heap on her. Shame washed over her, the horrible cycle of a terrible relationship so ingrained in her being that she hadn't even realized she was still going through it. "Maybe I'll have a third glass of wine. But I should go to bed early. I have to deal with Big Tag tomorrow. That requires all my faculties."

Sandra's face softened. "Big Tag is the easiest person in the world to deal with if you don't mind a little sarcasm. Honestly, he's the single most tolerant human being I've ever met."

"Are we talking about the same person?"

Sandra grinned. "Oh, he'll call out dumbassery wherever he sees it, but there's a kindness to the man if you look for it. Most of the things he does are because he gives a damn. Look, I think I know where you are."

"Dallas." She could be sarcastic, too, and she rather wanted to avoid this particular talk. One of the things she liked about Sandra was she kept things light.

But wasn't that what she'd wanted for years? Keep things light so she didn't have to get hurt again. Shallow friendships she didn't have to be honest about, didn't have to admit her flaws and mistakes because they were all about having a laugh.

Sandra ignored her. "My husband left me for a younger woman when Roni was five years old. I wasn't woman enough for him. His words, not mine. To him a woman was soft and feminine in a very traditional sense. Feminine to him meant wearing pretty clothes and ensuring his comfort and making him feel like a man because he wasn't strong enough to be one on his own. I made a mistake when I married him. I wouldn't take it back because I got two amazing kids out of the asshole, but he wasn't good enough for me. Now since then I've come to realize I'm good at being me. I like myself. I like being on my own. I don't think I'll ever get remarried, but I'm going to have a lot of fun before I go out. Sweetie, you aren't having fun."

"I wasn't married to him." To Roger.

"He still cost you a lot."

He'd cost her everything, including her self-esteem. "It was my fault. I was an Interpol agent and I didn't see that my partner, the man I was sleeping with, was working for the enemy, was using my work to help out his real boss."

And now that she was a year away from the fact, she could see how he'd distracted her. He'd used her own need-to-please nature against her.

Sandra sighed and put a hand on her arm. "No. That's where you're wrong. It wasn't your fault. You got used. You went into a relationship with all the right intentions. He was an asshole. Don't let him ruin the rest of your life. We're going to a beautiful tropical island soon. Think about finding some pleasure in it."

"I'm working. I'm there to find a corporate spy, not a shag."

"I don't see why you can't do both. As far as I can tell everyone else on the team has. It's kind of a thing they do," Sandra said, pulling her phone out of her pocket. "And I've seen some of the guys and ladies on staff. They are hot. You should consider it. I know I'm going to. I've got my eye on one of the bartenders. All of twenty-four. I can teach that boy something. But first, I've got a date."

Sandra hopped off her barstool.

It was easy to see her friend was making the most of her time now that her daughter and granddaughter were happily ensconced in their new home in Wyoming. Sandra had spent years protecting them after she'd lost her oldest child to a killer. She deserved every moment of pleasure she could get. Sandra had done everything right.

But she herself hadn't, had she? That was why she no longer trusted herself to do anything that wasn't on a rigid schedule. She made decisions based on a matrix she studied over and over to ensure she wasn't stepping out of line again.

She stopped. "I really am punishing myself, aren't I?"

Sandra slapped her on the shoulder. "Yes. You totally are punishing yourself, and that means the asshole wins. You know how he loses? If you have wicked-hot revenge sex. Not hate sex. Hate sex is something you would do with him, and then he gets to have an orgasm. No. you need revenge sex. Find someone hot and do him or her hard. Do that person until your eyes roll to the back of your head and you can't remember your name anymore. That kind of banging. Hey, there are actually a couple of really hot guys on the Dallas team. There's this guy named Boomer. Gorgeous. Not a brain in his head, but I would bet his dick works just fine. Buy him dinner and...well, he would probably follow you around for life. He really likes food. There are others. Michael. Hey, he's very sexy, and he's the son of our client for this mission."

She was not going there. "I do not shag where I eat. No. No one from McKay-Taggart, and definitely no one connected to Malone Oil. But I might think about the rest of it. Tell me about your man?"

Sandra's eyes went wide and she started to back up. "Not mine. I'm only playing with him for the night. They've got these apps now. Another great thing the young people have made. I can find a guy with a couple of swipes."

She shook her head. "Absolutely not. Online dating makes me...very ill."

"Not really dating. All right, my friend, I have to head out. I'm flying to the resort tomorrow afternoon with Hutch. We're getting out there early to set stuff up for our Agency contact. Vomit. I'll see you out there in a week. It's going to be fun to get some sun." Sandra slung her messenger bag over her shoulder. "Hey, you know there are a couple of single dudes here. Nothing wrong with dragging some tail out of a bar."

The waitress walking by had a sudden coughing fit.

Sandra had made it to the entrance and gave her a salute. "Use condoms."

How had Roni ever survived her teen years with Sandra as her mum? She waved as Sandra went off to find her fun for the evening.

"Your friend is funny." The bartender was shaking her head.

Despite the fact that the bar was attached to one of the more exclusive hotels in Dallas, it had a down-home feel. Oh, the drinks were expensive, but she didn't feel as out of place as she had in the lobby bar.

"She's very amusing." She also might be right. Was she letting Roger win? She'd been invited to dinner with Taggart and his group tonight. They were at a restaurant owned by Tag's little brother, and she would have met the whole team. Yet she'd told him she was getting in late and needed to rest. It was eight p.m. here, but it was two a.m. in London.

What she hadn't told him was she'd been preparing for the time difference for a solid week. She'd gradually adjusted her sleep time so she wouldn't feel the jet lag so keenly. She wasn't sleepy. She was perfectly awake and wondering if she would lie in bed like Sandra had guessed she would. She wasn't quite as bad as that. She would read an extra chapter from time to time.

She would lose herself in a sexy book because she refused to trust herself to find anything good in real life.

"If you were looking for someone to spend some time with, there's the single most gorgeous man I've ever seen in my life sitting behind you," the bartender said. "I would keep him for myself, but I don't swing that way. I was actually thinking about getting your friend's number, but then she intimidated me with the strap-on talk."

Sandra intimidated a lot of people. A lot. "I think I'll have this glass and then go upstairs."

The bartender shrugged. "All right, but that one is something special, and he has been checking you out."

Well, now she had to look. Didn't she? It wouldn't change anything. She would still do exactly what she'd planned. She would finish her second glass of wine, though she wasn't anywhere close to even being mellow, pay her tab, and go to her room where she would read the latest Kristen Ashley book until it was time to turn out the lights and go to bed.

This bloke wouldn't change a thing.

She turned her barstool slightly to the left, back to the tables that lined the window facing the street. There were several groups at the tables, but her eyes laser focused in on one. She'd briefly wondered if she'd be able to tell which man the bartender had been talking about. There were lots in here, and Texas men weren't exactly unattractive as a group. They tended to be quite masculine and lovely.

Oh, this was so much more.

Raven dark hair and a jaw carved from granite. Piercing eyes and broad shoulders, but beyond that there was an air of authority around the man. He would be the boss in whatever room he walked into, but he wouldn't force it. He wouldn't yell and bludgeon his way through. No. He would be quiet, and everyone would fall in line. Everyone would do his bidding, hoping the king smiled their way.

Hoping the king held out his hand and welcomed a commoner to join him. At his table. In his bed.

She'd been reading way too many romance novels.

"Yep, that's kind of the reaction I had, and I'm not even straight," the bartender replied with a chuckle. "He's been watching you. I've seen him in here a few times. I don't think he's married."

That was good for him and good for whatever woman he ended up taking to his room tonight because it absolutely wouldn't be her.

Why? Why not go over there and talk to him? Why not be bold and ask for the things she wanted? Did she have to be this pent-up, closed-off person she'd become forever, or could she take back a bit of herself?

All she would do was talk, spend maybe an hour with him if he was nice. She wouldn't go to bed with him. Probably not. Definitely not. He might not want to go to bed with her. But even if he did, she wouldn't. Probably.

Or maybe she would. Maybe she would give herself one night off from guilt and worry.

"I do believe I'm going in." She said the words out loud. "Should I take him a drink?"

The bartender quickly poured out a beer. "This is what he's drinking. And I'm here until close if you change your mind and need an easy way out."

She picked up both drinks and took a deep breath. It was time to see if she could claim a bit of herself back.

* * * *

JT Malone finished off his first beer of the night and turned his attention away from the gorgeous woman sitting with Sandra Croft. Not that Sandra wasn't nice on her own, but the woman next to her at the bar was simply stunning.

Her auburn hair was up in one of those loose buns women wore. He didn't think about hairstyles much, but there was something about her that made him want to walk up and ease her hair out of whatever band was holding it there so he could see it tumble around her shoulders. She was tall. Even sitting on a barstool he could tell she was likely five eight or five nine. Moments before, her lips had curled up at something Sandra had said, and her face had gone from lovely to knock-him-out gorgeous. That smile had rocked his world, and that was a bad thing.

Because she had to be Nina Blunt, and he was here for work, not play.

If he wasn't, he would get up and walk over to the bar and offer to buy her a drink. He would tell her she was the first woman in a very long time to intrigue him. Maybe it was because he did know a bit about her. Nothing personal beyond she was a badass and she lived in London. He knew she lived in a building that also served as a BDSM club. Did she play at The Garden? He'd gotten his Master rights at Sanctum months ago, but a brief relationship with his training partner hadn't gone anywhere, and he struggled to find vanilla dating interesting now.

He'd had his taste and he liked it. Naturally he needed something more. He had the damn world at his feet and he had to be picky. Pretty didn't do it for him. Strength did. He wanted a strong woman. One who could stand up to him, stand with him. A woman who could be a partner, take the lead when she needed to. And then obey him during sex.

Yep. He was a fucking keeper.

His cell phone vibrated and he glanced down, seeing his brother's name and picking up. "Hey."

"How's Dad?" Michael asked. "I'm sorry I couldn't get there today. I couldn't get out of here. The weather's bad. I've got an early flight in the morning."

"He's fine. The doctor said everything went perfectly and he'll be back to calling us all dumbasses in no time at all." It had been a day. A long, hard day. An emotional day, and he really hated getting emotional.

He'd thought he was going to lose his dad. He'd seen how pale his father had gotten, how he'd gritted his teeth against the pain in his chest. It was easy to think David Malone was immortal. He'd always been larger than life, but he wasn't going to be around forever, and the incident had forced him to look at his own life.

He was drifting, and not in a good way. He'd been numb for a very long time.

"Hey, are you all right?"

His brother had always known when he was on the edge. Even when they were thousands of miles apart, but then that was what being a twin meant sometimes. "I'm fine. It was a lot. He thought he was having a heart attack. Turned out to be his gall bladder. Apparently years of eating chicken fried steak has an effect. But they took it out with a laparoscope, and he won't even have much of a scar. Doc wants him to take it easy for a couple of weeks. Mom is in full-on warrior-queen mode, so I think he'll fall in line. The whole staff is dedicated to keeping him rested."

A chuckle came over the line. "That should drive him crazy. But seriously, I'm sorry you had to deal with that alone. I'll be out at the ranch as soon as I get back."

Their family home was a working ranch they'd grown up on. It was part of the business that was more about tradition than money. Malones had been in Texas long before it was a state, and the Circle M had been their home. Even after they'd started making their money off oil, they'd stayed on the ranch. Lots of people would have left the country for the wealth and luxury of the city, but not his father. No. His father still rode herd and fixed fences and woke his ass up before the crack of dawn so they could get ranch work in before they went to the office.

There were times he spent months on a rig just to get some damn sleep.

God, he'd thought he was going to lose his father, and then his father wouldn't ever know his wife or his kids. He shook it off.

"Good. They would love to see you, but I'm in Dallas and I'll be here until I head out to the island retreat." It was why he was here instead of at home, probably cursing at his dad because he would try to be active long before he should.

Unfortunately, corporate espionage didn't care that his father couldn't get on a plane anytime soon. The asshole who wanted to sell

Malone Oil's revolutionary tech to a foreign government didn't give a shit that JT Malone hated the very idea of a corporate retreat. If they canceled it, they lost the opportunity to catch a spy in the act. At least that was the way the CIA had explained it. He really did hate the bullshit that came with corporate retreats. He couldn't imagine how much he was going to hate one where he had to deal with the CIA, too.

Though it might not be so bad if he was able to get to know that gorgeous redhead. At least if his father was leaving him with a big problem, he'd also handed him a beautiful distraction.

"Whoa, we're going through with that? I thought the retreat was Dad's thing."

"It was Dad's thing and now it's mine." Like most of his world. That was what happened when a person was the heir to a multi-billion-dollar oil company. When his twin had decided to evade his fate by joining the military, it had all fallen on JT's shoulders. All of it. The business. His parents. The properties. The employees.

If his father had died…

There was a pause over the line. "I'll talk to Big Tag. You don't have to do this. I don't care what the Agency is saying. There will be another chance. You don't have to do their job."

Of course he did. If he didn't, the spy would set another drop location and they might not know where it was, might lose decades of innovation, and all because he didn't like to socialize. "Look, Mike, Dad's fine and we can't reschedule this retreat. Even if we did there's no guarantee the drop won't happen somewhere else." There was a throaty laugh and he glanced back at the bar. She was grinning from ear to ear as she laughed at something Sandra had said. Likely something very inappropriate. He'd only met the woman once before, but he'd heard tales from his brother of how she sometimes gave the big boss a run for his money in the sarcasm department.

"Then I should go. I can go in as you," Mike argued.

It wasn't anything he hadn't already thought of. He wasn't a spy. He hadn't spent years perfecting a poker face. He was known for speaking his mind. The last thing he wanted to do was play games.

Unless he was playing with her. Yeah, he could think of some games to play with her. They would involve rope and long hours of worshipping every inch of her skin.

He sighed and turned away again because he also wasn't the kind of man who fantasized about a woman he didn't even know. He was a realist. At least he was trying to be since being a romantic had gotten him nowhere. He would love to throw this all into Michael's lap since his brother had spent a decade learning the spy game.

But there was a major problem with this particular twin switcheroo. "It's a leadership retreat. Do you honestly believe you can fool people I've worked with for over a decade? We're going to be talking about work and new tech. These people know Malone Oil as well as our father, and you haven't been interested in a very long time. You can't conduct those meetings."

"You're also going to be hunting a spy," Michael countered.

He bit back a groan. He shouldn't have picked up the phone. All he and his brother seemed to do lately was bicker. "You didn't have a problem when it was Dad going in."

"Dad isn't reckless. Dad won't try to take down an international spy on his own."

He didn't seem to remember who their father was. "I assure you he's going to have a few things to say to whoever is selling out our corporate secrets."

"Yeah, but I trusted that Dad wouldn't go rogue in the middle of the investigation. He knows when to sit back and let the experts do their jobs."

Naturally his brother was ready, willing, and able to give him grief. "I assure you I'll let the lady bring down the bad guys."

"The fact that you call Nina a lady and not an operative is exactly what I'm worried about. You have to think of her as an operative. She doesn't need you to protect her, and that's what you tend to do. You'll like her. You'll be attracted to her, and that means you'll go into full-on protect-the-woman mode," his brother explained.

He couldn't help it that he was protective of the women in his life. It wasn't that he didn't think they were competent. They were. They were incredibly smart and he relied on them. But he knew what a man could do to a woman. "I can mind my manners."

"I wasn't criticizing. You know your manners are impeccable, and it's not wrong that you want to protect people, but it could make the job difficult on you." A sigh came over the line. "We can talk about this tomorrow. I'll come right to my condo and we'll discuss everything."

Oh, that was precisely why he'd decided to stay at the Adolphus. It hadn't merely been the fact that he'd been told by Big Tag's somewhat stern assistant this was where they were putting Nina Blunt up, though he'd thought they could talk about the change in the mission.

Or he could pretend he wasn't JT Malone. He could pretend he was just a guy and she was just a girl and maybe they would talk for a while. What could that hurt?

Or he could go to bed and deal with all of it in the morning. The weight of the world seemed to press on his shoulders.

"How about we talk in the morning?" He was so fucking tired.

"All right. If you need anything, call me."

"Will do." He hung up and slid the phone back into his pocket. He didn't want to look at it again. It was never anything but bad news lately.

He should go over and tell the gorgeous operative that she wouldn't be going in with his father. She would have to go in with him. Of course she might change her mind about taking the job if she talked to Mike. His brother—who she had almost certainly worked with and knew his opinion—thought he was a reckless moron.

She would likely think he was Mike at first since they were perfectly identical twins. Oh, if he took his shirt off, she would notice that he had scars Mike didn't have—deep gouges from working with barbed wire, a burn mark on his calf from not being careful enough on an oil rig. He didn't have Mike's gunshot scars. But if one was only studying faces, there was next to nothing that would tell them apart. How well did Nina and Mike know each other? McKay-Taggart was a big company and she worked in London while his brother was here in the States. It was possible they'd never met, but he was almost certain she would turn and see him and come over to talk about the fact that his company was the target of international spies and he better not fuck this up.

Maybe he should have gone straight to Mike's penthouse condo and raided his brother's Scotch. The beer wasn't doing much for him.

He needed something else. He needed to be out of his head for a while, but that wasn't going to happen.

He glanced up and saw Sandra had gone and Nina was looking right at him.

She quickly averted her eyes, but not before he saw the look in them. Like he was an ice cream cone and she hadn't had a sweet treat in so long.

Neither had he.

Fuck. She would definitely think he was Mike. Was she interested in his brother? Mike hadn't told him anything about her except that she was highly competent and selected because absolutely no one on the leadership team had come into contact with her, so her cover would be easy to keep. It was precisely why Sandra was going in as backup. She hadn't been with the company for long. McKay-Taggart had handled many of Malone Oil's security issues over the years, but Nina was fairly new to the London team and she'd never worked in the States before.

Had she caught sight of him staring at her? Would she be terribly disappointed to find out he wasn't his brother at all?

"Hi." She was standing in front of him, a glass of red wine in one hand and a beer in the other. "You looked like you could use another. Please tell me if I'm intruding. I don't want to bother you, but I'm a bit on the lonely side and you didn't seem to be waiting on anyone."

"I'm not." She wasn't talking like she knew him—or rather knew his twin. She was talking like a woman who'd seen someone she was interested in. "Please join me."

She smiled and he was utterly dazzled. "Thanks. It's been a long time since I chatted up a bloke. You'll have to forgive me if I'm terrible at it. I'm Nina."

He loved that accent. It was familiar since his mother had been born in England. She hadn't moved to the States until she'd married his dad. That accent oddly sounded like home.

He didn't want to say his name now because he liked the idea that he was nothing more than a guy in a bar and she was a woman who wanted to spend a little time with him. But he wasn't going to lie to her. "Jackson. But my friends call me JT."

She held out her hand. "Nice to meet you, JT."

There wasn't a hint of recognition in her eyes.

She had no idea who he was. None. She didn't know he was the heir to an oil company, had no clue he was considered one of America's most eligible bachelors, had been asked to star on reality shows where he would date twenty women and probably dump them all because no one should find their soul mate on national television. Which was why he'd turned them all down.

He was JT, a guy in a bar.

He reached for her hand and took it in his. "Nice to meet you, Nina. And I'm lonely, too. I appreciate the company."

It wouldn't hurt to pretend. Just for a little while.

# Chapter Two

Nina wasn't sure what she was doing, but she knew one thing. She didn't want to turn back and go to her own room. She'd spent the last two hours with JT. She didn't know his last name and didn't care. He didn't know hers, either. There was something freeing in being JT and Nina.

Not exchanging last names didn't mean she didn't know anything about him. She'd found out he worked for his father's company and his job took him all over the world. He was an utterly charming mix of down-home boy and sophisticated world traveler. He was a good listener. He had a brother and loved his family.

He was so sexy it hurt.

The lift doors opened and he held a hand out, allowing her to go first. He was also a perfect gentleman. After she'd bought him a beer, he'd bought the next round and then had made her choose between having another round or switching to coffee. She got the idea that if she'd had another drink, he wouldn't have invited her up to his room.

"Tell me something," she said as she moved to the elegant hallway. At this time of night, it was perfectly quiet. Her own room was several floors below. When the time had come to decide on whose room to go to, she'd insisted on his.

Yes, he was lovely, but she wanted an escape if she needed it.

"I've told you a lot. I can tell you more," he said in that deep Texas accent of his. He followed her off and the doors closed behind him.

She hoped she didn't need it. She hoped he was every bit the Cowboy Prince Charming he seemed to be.

"If I'd had drink number four, would we be here?" She was curious. She'd had more than one man try to ply her with drink to get what he wanted. It never worked, but she wanted to understand his reasoning.

He stared at her for a moment as though assessing the situation and then he leaned against the wall. "No. I would have made sure you got back to your room, but I don't know your threshold. I have zero interest in coaxing you with liquor. I would far rather know you wanted me and not some random guy to forget your troubles with. And I didn't want to get drunk either. Three's a good limit for me. I don't need anything to dull this experience."

He was forthright. She liked that quite a bit, and he hadn't had a fourth drink either. He'd been perfectly in control. Another thing she liked. She couldn't exactly come out and tell him she would very much enjoy it if he dominated her sexually. Or could she? "But I am trying to forget my troubles. That doesn't mean I don't want you in particular. If you hadn't been in the bar this evening, I would have settled for a book."

His lips curled up in the sexiest smile. "What kind of book?"

"Romance." Somehow she didn't think he would be derisive. Some people had contempt for the genre, but they were usually the ones who could use it the most.

He moved in, his hand coming up to brush a stray hair off her cheek, tucking it behind her ear. "I like the sound of that. It's your turn to tell me something. What would the hero of that book you would have read do right now?"

He'd backed her against the wall, but not in a way that felt threatening. He was taller than she was and loomed over her, his broad shoulders blocking most of her line of sight. She was still in her heels and for most men that put her at eye level or taller. Not with this one. It was nice to look up to a man for once. "I think he would invite her back to his room where they wouldn't shock anyone who happens to walk down the hallway."

He watched her like he was studying something fascinating, something he wanted desperately to learn. "I happen to know there are only two rooms on this floor, and I saw the couple in the other room go upstairs a few hours ago. They seemed like they were ready for sleep. Not that older couples can't party the night away, too, but they didn't seem like the type. So we don't have to worry about anyone catching us, though I'll be honest, I wouldn't be ashamed to get caught touching you."

He was pushing all her buttons. The good kind. The kind that got her in trouble. "So these are the penthouse suites?"

"Yes. My dad's company has an agreement with this hotel. We get priority for this suite. We do a lot of business in Dallas, though I don't live here. I live far enough on the other side of Fort Worth to make it hard to get home, so I stay here, and our suite was open."

His father's company must be ridiculously successful, but she wasn't going to get into that. Money was definitely not the reason she was interested in this hunk of cowboy. She had zero curiosity about his wallet. Now what he had in those jeans of his was another story altogether. "In that case, I suspect the hero would almost certainly kiss the heroine. He might press her against the wall and devour her. He might whisper all the things he's thinking of doing to her."

His eyes were on her mouth, as though he was thinking about doing exactly that. "Doing to her? What should I do to you, Nina? Should I take off your clothes? Should I unwrap you like the gift you are, taking my time because this is a present I didn't expect to get tonight? Should I unbutton that shirt you're wearing slowly, using every sense I have to catalog how gorgeous you are? Yes, I think that sounds like the way to go. I'll do it first by touch."

She was breathless as his fingers moved to unbutton the top two buttons of her blouse, brushing the skin he found there. He eased the sides back until he could see the tops of her breasts, a slight bit of her bra showing. She was damn glad she'd dressed for dinner with Sandra. She'd thought seriously about going the jeans and T-shirt route but at the last minute had wanted to look somewhat professional. A nice blouse meant a lacy bra.

"Soft, but then I knew your skin would feel like silk," he said, his voice deep.

A shiver of pure desire went through her and at that moment she wouldn't have cared if they'd been on the busiest floor in the building. He was all that mattered.

"After I've touched, I'll use my eyes to memorize the sight of you." He was staring down at the tops of her breasts. "You're beautiful." He reached out to trace the puckered scar that sat above her breast. "This is recent. Are you all right?"

It had been a couple of months since she'd taken a bullet from a German working against his country's best interests. Another corporate spy. "I mentioned I work for a security company in London. It was work related, but I'm fine. I don't want to talk about it, JT. Could we not?"

He seemed to want to press her, but he finally lowered his head. "Doesn't matter how you got it. It's part of you and still oddly lovely."

He gently kissed the scarred flesh. It seemed to come alive under his lips.

She brought her hands up to touch his arms, running from his elbows up to those shoulders that went on for days. It had been far too long since she'd had sex. That was why her whole body was a live wire waiting to go off. It wasn't merely the fact that JT seemed to know exactly how to touch her, the words to say to make her skin soften, the muscles loosening and readying.

"I'll use my lips," he continued. "I think that's what the hero would do. He would use his lips and tongue and teeth to explore."

He was going to drive her crazy. She was ready to get on her knees and submit to the man, if she didn't think that might freak him out. She would tell him that he should definitely use his teeth on her because she liked a bite of pain. Yes, she wasn't going there tonight. "He would definitely kiss me. I mean the heroine."

He lifted his head and brought his lips up to hover over hers. So close that she could feel the heat coming off him. "Would he? Would he put his mouth over hers and devour her like the starving man he is? Would he steal her breath? Would he plunge his tongue in like he's thinking of something else?"

Like his cock. "Yes. He would do all those things."

"See, I'm thinking I should read some of those books now. Much more pleasant than the ones I end up reading. No one ever kisses in engineering manuals. It's a mistake, I think." He lowered his head and brushed his lips along her mouth. "I'm supposed to know how to make things work, how to ease a machine this way or that so we get the best production out of it. All I want to do right now is find a way to make you melt for me."

He kissed her again, deeper this time, his tongue sliding along the seams of her lips, and she did exactly what he wanted. She melted, opening her mouth and letting him in. She felt his body move in as though he meant to capture every inch of territory she ceded to him. His tongue slid along hers, drawing her in and plunging deep. Showing her what he wanted to do with his dick.

She felt his hands moving from her neck down to her torso, one palm cupping her breast through her shirt. Her nipples peaked, getting hard and sensitive, and she wished there wasn't all that fabric between them. He pressed her against the wall and she let her hands roam across his muscled back and down to his ass, which was equally muscled. This man worked. Not merely worked out. He worked. It was there in the calluses on his fingers, which deliciously scraped along her skin. She loved the feel of those work-roughened hands smoothing back her blouse, exposing her to his eyes.

She got lost in his kisses. Drugged by the way the man couldn't seem to get enough. Over and over he kissed her, pulling her lower lip between his teeth and giving her a gentle nip that went straight to her pussy.

She needed more. More of him. More of his touch, more contact between them, more connection. She needed to get out of her skirt and blouse and show herself to him, see if he could handle what she needed.

His hands tugged at her skirt and she found herself pinned against the wall. His leg moved between hers.

"I want to watch you. I don't know that I'll be able to later," he growled against her ear. "Later, I'll be too far gone, so I want to watch you this once."

"Watch me?" She wasn't sure what he was doing, but he was even closer to her than before, their bodies in intimate contact.

"Watch you come." He moved and she was on his strong thigh, her toes barely touching the ground.

Her skirt was pushed up around her waist and she could feel the denim of his jeans starting to grind against her. The thin cotton of her underwear was absolutely no protection against the friction he was creating. But they were in the hall and she was off balance.

"Don't tense up." His voice had gone deep, commanding. "I've got you. I'm not going to let you fall, and I want you to stop worrying about anyone seeing us. It doesn't matter. Trust me. Come for me."

He was taking control in a way that did it for her. Even before she'd worked at The Garden, she'd known this was what she'd needed sexually. There was no backstory that had sent her looking for a dominant partner. That was something a lot of romance novels did get wrong. Oh, she knew some people who came to the lifestyle that way, but not the majority. It was simply how she was wired. She accepted it about herself, and that made it so easy to let him take control.

She relaxed and moved against him, matching the way he rubbed her, holding on to his shoulders as he found a rhythm. It didn't matter that her pussy was wet, her arousal likely seeping into the fabric of his jeans. It didn't matter that the lift doors could open at any minute. All that mattered was the heat and pleasure starting to build in her system.

"That's right. Take it. I want you to have it because I fully intend to be inside you the next time you come," he said. "We're going to go into my room and you're going to take off every stitch of clothing and offer yourself to me. You're going to be mine all night long."

She couldn't think of anything else she wanted to be. His. All night. For a single night she didn't have to worry about the mistakes of the past or what she might do with her future. All that would matter was letting this man bring her pleasure, finding joy in bringing him some, too.

Sandra had been so right. She needed this. It was a night off from more than work. It was a night off from being the martyr she'd become. With JT she didn't have to be the woman who'd fucked up her whole career. She could be nothing more than a partner in bliss.

He pressed up, and the pressure that had been building exploded in the best of all ways. She held on to him, looking him in the eyes as she took everything he gave her.

It was one of the most intimate experiences of her life.

"That's what I wanted." JT eased her down until her feet were on the floor. But not for long. He almost immediately leaned over and picked her up like she weighed nothing at all. Her shoe fell off, but he turned anyway. "I'll get it for you later, Cinderella. Now it's my time."

She didn't care about the shoe. The shoe could get lost. All that mattered was more of him.

* * * *

His dick was dying, but it would have to wait because if there was one thing JT knew, it was that he wasn't going to let this woman get away from him. She was fascinating and he wanted to spend time getting to know her, seeing if they could work. Suddenly the mission he had to go on seemed more like a blessing than a curse.

Except she didn't know she was going on the mission with him. She didn't know his father had to stay home and her primary contact was now him.

He glanced down at the woman in his arms as he managed to get the door to the suite open. She looked happy and languid, her hair mussed and lips slightly swollen from his kisses.

He'd put that look on her face. He had zero doubt she would be competent in the field. She would command a team while she was working, and he planned on letting her call all the shots on this op. He would be her way in, arm candy so to speak, but when they were alone, it would be his time and he would be in charge. He would indulge her on every level, learn what she liked and give it to her, but in the bedroom, she would obey him.

That was how he would keep her. Give her more pleasure and attention than any other man had ever given her. They would have a couple of weeks before she went back to London. A few weeks to show her how it might be between the two of them. A try-out affair to see if they had a future.

"This place is gorgeous. Was that a pool table?"

Actually, it was, and it might be perfect for what he wanted to do to her. They would eventually make it to the bedroom, but that pool table was the right height. He turned and strode back. "This is a massive suite for one man, but it was a last-minute thing. I've got a meeting tomorrow afternoon that I hadn't counted on. This was the easiest place for me to stay. Usually we put up executives and their families here."

"What business is your father in?"

He shook his head. He wasn't going to have her put on her investigator hat tonight. She'd find out soon enough in the morning. "Nope. No business talk tonight. You didn't want to talk about work. Neither do I."

He didn't want to lose her. He knew damn well why she'd wanted to come up to his room instead of going to hers. She was a smart lady who wanted an out if she needed one. He didn't intend to give her a reason to leave.

He set her on the edge of the pool table, her legs dangling off. It was dark but he didn't want to turn on the lights. The staff had been in for turndown service, but he'd stayed here enough to know the best way to illuminate this particular room. It might also get her mind off what he did for a living. He walked to the window and pulled open the drapes, letting the lights of the city wash the room in color.

She gasped and a smile crossed her face. Not a sexy smile, though he still found her sexy. No, this was a smile of wonder. He moved to the second window and opened those floor-to-ceiling drapes and let the night in.

"Wow. That's beautiful." She slipped off the pool table. Her skirt had slid back down her thighs and she'd kicked off her other shoe. Her hair had come down around her shoulders. She hadn't bothered to rebutton her shirt, so he could see a creamy expanse of skin as she joined him by the windows. A light rain streaked the glass and the world seemed softer than it had before he'd walked into that bar.

She was the beautiful one. While she looked out over the neon city, he watched her. With her shoes off, she would fit perfectly right under his chin as he cuddled her close. If she danced with him, she could easily lay her head against his chest while they swayed to the music.

"It's like the whole city is laid out for us," she said, her palms against the window.

He moved behind her, letting his hands find her waist and moving to her hips. "I want you laid out for me."

She turned and her fingers went to the buttons of her blouse. Her expression had gone serious, her eyes heating as she looked at him. Slowly, she undid the little pearl-like buttons, easing the shirt off. She let it drop to the floor. It left her in a cream-colored bra that pushed her breasts up and held them in lace like the jewels they were.

"Take it off for me, Nina."

Her hands went to the clasp of the bra, twisting and releasing it before she offered it to him. He took it and her shirt, draping them both on the back of the sofa. This room was part library, part game room, but tonight it would be all about pleasure. "The rest of it. I told you what I wanted."

"Yes, sir."

She couldn't know what that word did for him. Years of his life he'd spent not understanding what he needed from a partner. It was one of the best things that had come from Mike up and leaving him alone to take care of their family. He'd been invited to Sanctum because of Mike, and that had made a huge difference in his life. It taught him what he needed, what made him happy. What eased his soul.

Something settled deep inside him as she slid her skirt off and then dispensed with the lacy underwear that covered her. When she stood in front of him completely naked, trust in her eyes, he knew this was going to go beyond anything he'd had before.

He stepped up to her, letting his hands cup her shoulders and bringing her hair around so it hung down in auburn tresses that skimmed the tops of her breasts. He traced a line from her neck down to one tight nipple.

"Tell me what you like."

"I like you." She didn't move, didn't press herself up so he touched more of her. She simply stood there as though content to wait. "I'll likely like anything you do, JT. You know those romances I like to read? A whole lot of them are kinky."

Fuck. His groin tightened, and he wasn't sure his dick could get any harder. She was offering herself up to him in the sweetest of ways, and he was determined to stay in control. "Then go sit on the pool table."

She hesitated. "JT, I'm not exactly…how to describe this…"

It was obvious what she was talking about. He leaned in close and moved his hand to touch the mound of her pussy, to slide through all the delicious cream he found there. She'd had an orgasm and it coated her. It also was making her hesitate for fear of getting something messy.

Wealth had its privileges. "Don't worry about the pool table. Don't worry about the staff having to clean up. Don't worry about anything but how we can make each other feel. Now sit on the pool table and spread your legs for me."

"You want to be in control of this, don't you?"

"I do," he replied. "I want you to let me take control. I want you to trust me with your body and your pleasure."

For a moment he worried she would walk to the sofa and get her clothes. That he'd misread her. But she crossed the room and gracefully placed herself on the edge of the elegant pool table. He'd stayed here many times, had played at that table while he talked business and drank Scotch in that good old boy way things tended to work in his world, but he would never be able to be in this room again without seeing her sitting there.

She slowly, carefully, spread her legs. "Better?"

So much better. Perfect. She was fucking perfect.

He pulled his shirt over his head and tossed it on the sofa with hers. He was prepared. Always a Boy Scout, he had a condom in his wallet, and he'd moved it to his pocket when he'd realized where this was going. He crossed the space between them and placed it on the edge of the pool table.

Then he moved between her open legs, making a place for himself there. It was right where he wanted to be, where he needed to be. He wanted to be naked with her, but he couldn't risk it yet. He still had things he needed to do to her, to show her how he could worship her body.

He kissed her, tangling his fingers in her hair and using them to hold her where he wanted her. A little shudder went through Nina, accompanied by a low moan that let him know she'd liked that twist he'd given her hair. Naturally this was the woman he connected to, the one he shouldn't have.

Was absolutely going to have.

He would deal with the ramifications later. Tonight, all that mattered was making her his. She didn't know it, but she was going to be his for a lot longer than a night.

He tangled their tongues together, loving the way she moved with him. It was easy to kiss Nina, like they'd done it a thousand times before. There was nothing awkward about kissing her, just an easy sensation that told him this was right.

He moved from her mouth, kissing along her jaw and down her neck. He kissed a path to her breast, easing over the scar he was certain was a bullet wound. It reminded him that she was here to do a job.

He would have the story of how she got that bullet wound. He would have all her stories in the end.

But for now he would settle for something other than words coming out of her mouth.

He licked her nipple, tonguing the tight bud before sucking it between his lips.

A shudder and a moan went through her and her hands moved to the table behind her, balancing her. It had the added plus of thrusting those gorgeous breasts his way, making it easier for him to lavish them with affection. He moved from one to the other, taking in how her breath hitched, the way she squirmed when he gave her the edge of his teeth.

"You like that." He nipped her, biting down just so she could feel it.

A sweet moan came from her. "I do."

He nipped her again and then dropped to his knees. Yes, the table put her at exactly the right height for what he wanted to do. "I suspect you'll like this, too."

He spread her knees even farther apart and leaned in. That was one gorgeous pussy. He could see the pink bud of her clitoris swollen and poking out of its hood after her recent orgasm. The little pearl needed even more affection.

"Do you think you'll like this, Nina?" He liked saying her name. He liked it even more when she was staring down at him, her lower lip between her teeth and heat plain in her gaze.

"Oh, please. Please, JT."

Well, he didn't like to disappoint a lady. He leaned in and kissed her, letting her scent wash over him. It was better than any perfume. It was her essence, her arousal. He could bathe in that scent and be perfectly happy.

And her taste. It coated his tongue. He parted her labia, settling on her clitoris as he eased his finger inside. She was tight but slick with arousal. She would take him easily, but he wanted to give her more.

"I want you to come on my tongue," he said against the warm flesh of her pussy. "Do you understand me, Nina?"

"Yes," she replied in that heavenly accent of hers. So polished and educated. He loved the fact that he could make that accent go deep.

He thrust in and out with his finger, curling deep inside her and looking for the perfect spot to make her go off like a rocket. She was primed and ready for another orgasm.

He was the man to give it to her.

His blood thrummed through his system as he focused every bit of his being on her. This was what was missing from his other sexual encounters. He'd always been able to hold a bit of himself back, but he wanted to drown in this woman. He lost himself in her taste, the soft feel of her flesh, the sounds of her crying out as he found the perfect rhythm.

He kept it up until she shuddered and fell back against the table.

He got to his feet, licking the taste off his lips. He wouldn't get enough of her. Not tonight. Maybe never. She was different.

He shoved his jeans down. Next time he would get naked with her, but this would do for now. He couldn't hold back a second longer. He needed to get inside her. He stroked his cock and rolled the condom on as he stared down at her. She was the very picture of lush femininity, with her skin flushed and her eyes half closed, her hair tousled in a halo around her head. The lights from the city played on her skin, and he memorized her in the moment.

She reached a hand up. "I want to be with you."

He pulled her up and to him until their chests were bumping and mouth fusing again. Her legs wrapped around his waist, arms enclosing him, and when she shifted, he could feel his dick against her pussy.

"Yes, that's what I want," she whispered against his lips.

"It's everything I want." He found the globes of her ass, lush and soft, and used the leverage to force his cock inside.

Pleasure swamped his senses. She was tight around him as he eased out and thrust back in. "You feel perfect to me."

Her head fell back and her eyes closed as if she couldn't quite keep them open. "Your cock feels like heaven."

Even through the physical pleasure, he heard her words and they did something for him. Women wanted him for different reasons, but always underneath all of it lay the fact that he was the heir to Malone Oil. No matter what, that fact was between him and his lover. Most of the women in his life wanted something from him. Nina wanted his cock. Nina wanted his affection.

He could give all of it to her.

He let himself go, thrusting in again and again. She held on to him, wrapping him up in the heat and silk of her body. He held on to her as she shook in his arms, and then it was his turn. He let the pleasure wash over him.

He kept her wrapped up even as he started to come down from the high.

He knew one thing. He wasn't going to let her go.

# Chapter Three

Nina stared at herself in the mirror, the bathroom still steamy from her shower. She'd made a major mistake the night before. She'd thought she could wake up this morning and walk away from that gorgeous, sexy, affectionate man without a backward glance and now she knew the truth.

She was half in love with the man and had zero desire to never see him again. It was going to be hard to wait the thirty minutes or so before he came back with their breakfast. He'd called down and room service had said there was a problem with the kitchen and it would be at least an hour and a half before they could send someone up. JT had claimed he couldn't wait and promised her cheap breakfast sandwiches combined with expensive coffee.

He'd kissed her before he'd gone and asked if they could talk when he got back. He'd told her he didn't care that she lived in London. He wanted to see her again.

She dried off and thought briefly about going downstairs to her own room and getting dressed but it seemed like a long way to go. Instead she slipped into JT's T-shirt and wound one of the hotel's robes around her body.

The better to seduce him with. She could toss these off in seconds and be ready for round number four.

Two the night before. He'd woken her up with sex this morning. Fourth time was the charm.

She had a week before the retreat, though she would have to work most of the time. Then she would be gone for a week, but she would likely have to return to Dallas for the debrief. She hadn't used any vacation time. She might be able to talk her boss into giving her some. A holiday.

Just to see if what they'd found the night before was something they could build on.

And she would ask for his last name. They were definitely ready to move on to last names.

She should check her phone. She had a few hours, but it wouldn't hurt to check in with the office. The meeting wasn't until this afternoon when she would get to meet her partner for the next two weeks. David Malone. Apparently he was the father of one of the Dallas office's agents. She'd never met Michael Malone, but she knew him by reputation.

It had sounded like such an easy assignment. Learn a bit about the petroleum business and the Malone family. Take the nice Texas oil man to a tropical paradise, pretend to be his new assistant, and catch whoever was selling out the company to foreign interests. Easy peasy, and she could work on her tan while she did it.

Now she wanted to stay here and see her cowboy. The question was could she do her job during the day and see him at night? She was supposed to immerse herself into learning the business and the Malones, but there should be some personal time, right?

She stopped. Was she doing it again? Was she letting herself get so wrapped up in a man that she gave up everything for him?

This was exactly what had happened before. With Roger.

JT wasn't Roger. She couldn't put that stamp on every man for the rest of her life. Nina took a deep breath as she walked into the room with the pool table. In the light of day, the suite was even more impressive than it had been the night before.

She was pretty sure her entire flat could fit into this one. Morning light filled the room and washed over the pool table where she'd been worshipped the night before.

JT was the best lover she'd ever had. Was she mistaking good sex for emotion?

Her clothes were strung over the sofa along with the ones he'd been wearing the night before. She picked them up, folding them all.

She took a deep breath and decided to stop panicking, stop overthinking. She would go with the flow. There was nothing wrong with enjoying the morning together, and then when she got back from the job, she would give him a call and maybe they could have another night together and go from there.

She stared out over the city, her mind on the man walking

somewhere below. What was he thinking? He'd said he wanted to talk. Somehow she didn't see JT wanting to talk about how the sex had been good, but they should go their separate ways. No. He was going to suggest they see each other again.

That was how she would play it. She would agree to date him when she had time off work, and they would take it from there. She wouldn't throw herself wholly into a relationship. Cool. She would play it cool.

Her cell trilled and she turned away from the morning light with a sigh. Maybe having a week away from JT would give her some perspective. She could spend the week reminding herself that one night did not a relationship make. Sandra would be good at helping her through this. Sandra would be ridiculously over-the-top honest with her. If she called her friends back in London, they would look at the whole situation through a romantic lens. That was because all her friends back in London were happily married and cranking out babies like they were trying to populate the world.

Did JT want kids?

What was wrong with her? She growled as she picked up the phone. Yes, work would be good. Work would remind her that the world wasn't some romance novel. Work would remind her that if she didn't pay attention, she would get shot again, and she didn't need any more scars. "Good morning, Sandra."

"Oh, you did not take my advice." She could practically see Sandra shaking her head. "You sound even more tense than you did before, and what I have to tell you isn't going to help."

"In fact, I did take your advice. I shagged the most delicious man I've ever seen in my life, and it was fabulous. So fabulous that if I were a schoolgirl, I would have spent the morning writing my married name in a notebook and planning our wedding. If I knew his last name."

A chuckle came over the line. "Ah, so that's what's crawled up your backside this morning. See, that's your problem. You went for a thoroughbred when you should have started with something a little less sleek. You gotta build up to really good sex when you're young. I'll pick your guy next time."

She sank down to the sofa. "That's the problem. I think I want to see him again. We're supposed to talk when he gets back."

"You're still there? Damn, girl. You know you're supposed to run as fast as possible. We're going to have to work on your one-night-stand style."

The last thing she wanted was a one-night-stand style. She needed to find a happy medium between plowing through dicks and getting far too attached to the first dick she saw.

It had been a really lovely dick.

"I promise it won't make me late. I'm not due in the office until one. Big Tag thinks far too much of jet lag, but this time it works in my favor. I've got plenty of time to review the dossier on Mr. Malone. I've memorized the ones on our most likely suspects."

They included two members of the senior leadership team and an admin attached to David Malone's son. The admin was going in her boss's place. Apparently Jackson Malone wasn't big on retreats.

Jackson.

The name seemed very popular here in Texas.

"Well, our op took a left turn," Sandra said. "David Malone had emergency surgery yesterday and he can't travel for a few weeks."

Fuck. "Is Tag scrubbing the op?"

It would be hard to explain her presence without David Malone. She could work it from a staff angle, the way Sandra was, but there was a reason they'd been trying to do both.

"Nope. You're going to go in with David's son. We're bringing JT Malone in this afternoon so we can lay the groundwork for your new cover. He's already got an admin. She'll be going along, but we can't tell her the truth because she's under suspicion."

She stood up at the sound of those initials coming from Sandra's mouth. "Excuse me."

Surely she'd heard wrong.

"She's been his admin for a long time," Sandra explained. "I don't know JT the way I do his brother, Michael…"

"Did you say JT?" She paced the floor, the signs she should have seen the night before becoming plain now.

David Malone lived on the other side of Fort Worth on a ranch called the Circle M. Just far enough to make staying in Dallas necessary at times. Staying in a fabulous suite that was available to him and his son. He'd said something about engineering. She'd thought he did something mechanical, but he could be a petroleum engineer.

No.

No.

Fucking no.

This could not be happening to her. She did not sleep with the client.

She picked up her clothes because she might need some armor to deal with this situation.

"Yeah, that's David's son. JT Malone. He's hot, too," Sandra said. "I only know that because Mike is his twin. See, now there's a thoroughbred. I know I joked about hooking up with him, but he's probably a tidal wave of sex. You need the kiddie pool. JT's not married either, so I'll get a chastity belt for you. Maybe you should go in as a lesbian. We could do the couples thing. I've heard it used to work for Jake and Adam."

JT had absolutely been a tidal wave, and she'd ridden him all night long.

A little panic threatened. She didn't sleep with people she had to work with. Ever. Well, not since that first time when she'd been used to feed an arm's dealer Interpol intelligence.

She was going to get fired. Her job was all she had.

Unless JT met with an accident. She knew several assassins, and quite frankly a couple of them owed her favors. Tucker was a doctor. Maybe he still had some of that forget-everything medicine. She wasn't sure if she would use it on JT or herself.

Fuck.

"Nina?" Sandra asked.

A chiming went through the suite, the doorbell.

JT was back and now they really needed to talk since she was going to have him murdered. She liked him and she would also probably lose her job if she killed the client. They had to make this work.

There wasn't time to prep someone else. They would need a good cover. She could be his cousin or something. David Malone's wife was English. That could work. Absolutely. She could handle this. JT would be reasonable because this was his business at stake.

"Sandra, I have to go." She wouldn't tell anyone. Not even Sandra. She and JT would make a pact to be utterly silent about the events of the previous evening.

About the sex. About the incredible sex that had felt like something more.

She took a deep breath and hung up the phone. She was panicking over absolutely nothing, and honestly, panic was beneath her.

Had she panicked when the red notice criminal she'd been arresting had tossed a bomb her way? No. She'd lobbed that bloody bomb right back at the bastard and saved her partner in the process. She could handle sleeping with the wrong man.

Except he'd been the right man, and her whole body had known it.

Still, there was nothing to do now except find a professional level with a man she knew could rock her whole world. She wouldn't think about how his hands felt on her body or the fact that no one in the world had ever eaten her pussy quite as thoroughly as JT Malone. No. He was a client now and she would let him back in, explain the situation, and then go get dressed because she couldn't be professional when she was wearing his T-shirt and luxuriating in his scent.

She opened the door. "JT, we need…"

Two men in business suits and a well-dressed woman stood in the doorway. The woman appeared to be in her late twenties or early thirties, and her eyes narrowed as she took Nina in.

"What the hell are you doing…" She huffed, a long-suffering sound, and she brushed by Nina, handing her the shoe that had fallen off in the hall the night before. "Looks like you forgot something. Drunk much?" She turned back to the men she'd come with. "Come in. She's some chick JT dragged out of a bar last night. JT!"

Maybe she would murder someone today. She knew exactly who that angry little woman was. Deanna Kilgore, assistant to the vice president in charge of pretty much everything. She'd studied the woman's dossier but glanced over her boss since her boss was considered above reproach and therefore uninteresting to her.

If only she'd paid attention to Deanna's boss, maybe she wouldn't have slept with him.

Unfortunately, the other two intruders completed her list of horrors. Jordan "Jordy" Burton, board member and all-around adventurer, and Patrick Franks, who served as the VP of operations of Malone Oil. They were her entire list of suspects. She recognized every one of them, and now they would recognize her, too.

The whole operation was on the line. The reason they'd brought her in was the fact that no one from Malone Oil could possibly know who she was. The whole job would have to be scrubbed, and there was every likelihood JT's company would suffer for it.

"He's not here." She said the words even as her mind raced, looking for a solution. She had to be at that retreat. If they missed this opportunity, the Agency would force Malone Oil to admit what was happening to the press and cause a major scandal that would hurt their bottom line for decades. It was precisely why most companies didn't prosecute corporate spies. "He went out for coffee."

She stayed at the door, hoping they would go back out the way they came.

"I'm not leaving until I talk to him," Jordy insisted. He was a well-built man. The expensive suit he was wearing didn't hide his muscles, though she knew he'd gotten them in a gym. He was a trust-fund baby, though apparently he'd blown through much of it. "That email yesterday was complete bullshit."

Patrick was on his heels. He was ten years older than Jordy, and his background was far less privileged. It was his ties to Russian companies that made the Agency interested in him. "I agree. I'm a member of senior leadership. I expect more than *David Malone will not be attending our retreat.* I have every right to know what happened, Deanna. You said JT would be here. You didn't tell me he was shacked up with a hooker."

"I'm his girlfriend, and you might think twice about insulting me." The words were out of her mouth before she could really consider the ramifications of them. Although since they'd caught her in his room wearing nothing but his shirt, she wasn't sure they would buy the cousin angle she'd so recently come up with.

The retreat was open to families and loved ones. JT could bring his girlfriend.

Oh, he was going to be the one to murder her. She was going to have to explain to the poor man how his one-night stand had turned into a relationship.

"You are not his girlfriend," the admin said, hands on her hips.

"Don't be so coy, baby," a masculine voice said. "Nina here is far more than my girlfriend. She's my fiancée. I know we didn't want to tell anyone until we could have a party, but after what happened with Dad last night, I don't think we can wait."

She turned and JT walked in like the fact that a good portion of his office was standing in his suite didn't bother him at all.

What had he said? Fiancée? Oh, god, she'd just become a fake fiancée to a billionaire.

And now everyone would know. Including her boss.

The night before had been good sex, but this was what it meant to be truly fucked.

\* \* \* \*

JT figured out things had gone heinously wrong the minute he set foot off the elevator and turned down the hall that led to his half of the floor. The door was open and he could hear voices up ahead.

"I'm not leaving until I talk to him. That email yesterday was complete bullshit."

JT winced. Jordy was here, and that likely meant Deanna had tracked him down. Jordy wouldn't have been able to do it by himself. JT had ignored her texts the prior day. He'd been at the hospital and he hadn't needed his overly ambitious admin's bullshit. For the most part Deanna was perfect. She did everything he didn't want to do and was an excellent gatekeeper. One day she would move into an executive position and she would be damn good at it.

But she had boundary issues. Like she didn't think there should be boundaries closed to her when it came to him. He'd sent her a terse email telling her he had a family emergency and would call her last night.

Then he'd met Nina and he'd let everything go. Obviously that decision was going to come back to haunt him today.

"I agree." Patrick's cultured voice grated on JT's nerves at times. "I'm a member of senior leadership. I expect more than *David Malone will not be attending our retreat.* I have every right to know what happened, Deanna. You said JT would be here. You didn't tell me he was shacked up with a hooker."

Oh, he was about to haul Patrick out and toss him to the street. How fucking dare he…

Nina was going to be upset, and she had every right to be. He hadn't figured out how he was going to tell her they were working together. He meant to. He'd considered telling her about his meeting at McKay-Taggart and oops, what, she was going there, too?

He hadn't meant for her to find out because his admin and a couple of members of his board showed up and started calling her a hooker.

And honestly, he didn't like the term hooker. He'd worked in some crazy parts of the world, places where there were almost no women due to the nature of the work, and sex professionals made life way easier. They were nice women who did a good job.

Yeah, he probably shouldn't have that argument in front of Nina. She would already be angry. Was this going to screw up the job? He could hear his brother now. He was going to fuck up the op and his relationship with Nina.

"I'm his girlfriend and you might think twice about insulting me."

He took a deep breath because that had been said with pure confidence.

"You are not his girlfriend." Deanna had some confidence of her own, but he could work with this. He'd been out of the office for months, allowing her to deal with all the paperwork and inner-office stuff while he was going from rig to rig testing out the new equipment.

She had no idea what he'd been doing with his personal life. No one did.

Nina was smart. She'd played the only card she could since he knew damn well how important it was that the agent he went in with had a good cover. They might have been able to go with bodyguard.

But girlfriend worked fine for him. In fact, he could take it one step further since those assholes would likely treat her like crap if they thought he wasn't serious about her. He rounded the corner and caught sight of her standing in the doorway, holding it open like she still might be able to force them to leave.

He knew better.

"Don't be so coy, baby." He strode in, coffee and breakfast in hand. He winked her way before turning to their unwanted guests. It didn't escape his notice that she had her clothes from the night before over her arm when they'd agreed she would be naked and waiting for him this morning. "Nina here is far more than my girlfriend. She's my fiancée. I know we didn't want to tell anyone until we could have a party, but after what happened with Dad last night, I don't think we can wait."

"You're not engaged." Deanna had a shocked look on her face that told him she was genuinely emotional.

Damn. His mother had called that one. His mom had told him to watch Deanna because she was far too invested in their personal relationship. He'd assured her they didn't have one, but it looked like his admin didn't agree.

Well, then Nina could help him out with that because he needed to keep those boundaries firmly in place.

"I assure you she is." He set the coffees on the counter along with the breakfast sandwiches and pastries he'd gotten since he didn't know if she preferred savory or sweet. He reached a hand out to her. "Unless you changed your mind, baby. You still going to marry me?"

She didn't miss a beat, taking his hand and letting him haul her close. "Not a chance, cowboy."

He lowered his lips to hers and could feel the stiffness in her body, though she welcomed the kiss readily. "I love it when you tease me."

"No." Deanna paced the floor of the suite. "This is some kind of joke. You aren't even dating anyone."

He needed to get Nina up to date and fast. He kept her hand in his as he faced the intruders. "I met Nina through a friend of my mother's. I was headed out to Loa Mali to an engineering conference and I had a few days. I spent them with her. As you know I've been on the road for six weeks. Nina has come out to be with me whenever she could."

"You were on oil rigs," Deanna pointed out.

"Oil rigs still have private rooms," Nina shot back, placing a hand on his chest. "Trust me. If you want to get to know a man, spend three days on a rig with him. You find out a lot about his habits."

That hand felt awfully possessive. Yes, this could work out perfectly for him. "Hey, I took you to Loa Mali on a private plane. It wasn't all bad."

She went up on her toes. "I'm going to get dressed. I didn't think I would have to meet your coworkers until we got to the retreat. I'm going to change."

She winced slightly as though she realized the mistake she'd made.

"I'll get rid of them," he promised.

He tilted his head down and she came up to brush her lips against his.

"I'll explain. I promise," she whispered.

She thought he was way smarter than he was. Or more trusting. Fuck. He couldn't tell her he'd known why she'd said what she said. He needed a plan or she would walk out on him and then he would lose the girl and his father would be angry he'd screwed everything up.

But first, he had to deal with the snakes in his suite. It did not escape him that every one of them was on the Agency's list. He couldn't see it. He knew that trio could be hard to take at times. Still, he couldn't see them betraying not only the company but the country. However, figuring out who was the spy was Nina's job and he was going to let her do it.

If he could pull off the fiancée thing. He nodded and she strode off to the bedroom—after she took her coffee and the bag of breakfast goodness.

He turned to the intruders, and he didn't have to pretend to be irritated. He fucking was irritated. "You want to explain why I'm not having a very nice morning with the woman I'm going to marry?"

"You want to explain how you're marrying a woman no one has

met?" Deanna asked. "I don't buy this, JT. What the hell is going on?"

"I don't give a damn about what you want to do with your romantic life. I want to know what's going on with David Malone," Jordy said.

"Why isn't he going on the retreat?" Patrick stood behind Jordy. "He hasn't missed the retreat in twenty years. Your email said something about his health. Did he have a heart attack? Because we have the right to know if the CEO of the company is on death's door."

"And how could you send out that email?" Deanna complained. "That should never have gone out. We have people to do that. People who know how to word things so you don't spark a bunch of rumors that could potentially tank our stock."

He winced. "Yesterday was rough. I didn't think about it. I'm sorry. My father is fine. He had his gallbladder out. His recovery time is minimal, but he needs to take it easy for a few weeks."

Deanna's shoulders came down from around her ears. "All right. I'll write up a brief report and I'll handle the press. I was already going to the retreat, so I can get you up to date on everything very quickly." She frowned. "I made your father's travel arrangements. He said he was bringing a new assistant with him. Her name was Nina, too."

Fuck. He was not a damn spy. "Yeah, Dad wanted to ease Nina into the business part of our world, and he thought the retreat would be the perfect place to do it. The fact that she's also his future daughter-in-law isn't really anyone's business. I'm sure it would have come up, but he wasn't going to make a big deal out of it. It was also going to be a good way to spend time with her. Instead she got to sit in a hospital room and listen to my parents bicker about how long he would have to stay in bed. Now, if you don't mind, we drove out here to Dallas late last night so we could get everything we need for the retreat. I'll be in the office tomorrow if you need anything. I've got a meeting with our security company at one, and I would like to spend some time with my fiancée. Deanna, do all the things you need to do, starting with getting these two out of my suite."

She looked like she wanted to argue, but she simply nodded. "Gentlemen, you have your answer."

"I don't have any proof," Patrick replied. "He could be lying."

Deanna stepped in between them, which was a good thing because he was about to show Patrick how he handled assholes.

"He's a terrible liar," Deanna said with a tight smile. "Trust me. I would know if he was lying. We've reached the end of his patience. You have your answer. Let's get back to the office."

She sent him a look that let him know this wasn't over.

He closed the door behind them.

"I can explain." Nina was standing in the doorway to the bedroom, a worried look on her face. She'd put on her clothes from the night before and despite a few wrinkles, looked all buttoned up again.

It was not how he wanted to spend his morning. He needed more time with her.

He held up his phone. "You're Nina Blunt. You work for McKay-Taggart."

She let out a sigh of obvious relief. "They sent you an email with my dossier."

Yep. He'd read it the day before, but she didn't need to know that. "I guess we have a lot to talk about."

She shook her head and walked around him to get her shoes. "We do, but I got a call from my boss. The CIA agent we're going to be working with is in town and wants to meet right away. I need to get to the office. Perhaps we can talk later this afternoon. We can definitely talk about how this is going to work. Girlfriend would have been easier than fiancée, but we have to go with it now. You need to contact your parents in case the assistant decides to ask about our out-of-nowhere engagement."

"They'll treat you better if they think you're going to be a member of the family," he said.

"You shouldn't concern yourself at all with how they'll treat me." She managed to make what should have been a suggestion sound like an accusation. "I can handle whatever they throw at me."

There had been another reason for him changing her plan. "I probably wouldn't bring a girlfriend to something like this, and my employees would know that."

She nodded as she slipped into her heels. "All right. Well, we'll need a good cover. We can discuss it at the office."

"Or we could talk about it over dinner," he suggested. He could see the *no* on her face, but he had a counter. "We need to spend time together. Look, I know this is weird, but I was coming back up here to ask if I could see you again. I don't see how this changes anything at all except that we don't have to take a week or two before we go on an actual date."

Her eyes widened and she grabbed her purse. "It changes everything, Mr. Malone."

Oh, she was upset, and he wasn't sure what that was about. He only knew he wasn't going to let it stand. But he could give her some space. For now. "I look forward to seeing you this afternoon, Ms. Blunt."

She rushed out the door and he admired her very lush backside as he pulled out his cell phone and dialed his brother's number.

"Hey, I just got off the plane. Everything okay?" Mike asked.

"I slept with my McKay-Taggart contact and she's freaked out about it." It was best to own up to everything when it came to his brother. "And you're going to tell me why."

He could do his research, too.

After his brother stopped cussing.

# Chapter Four

"All right, everything is ready and you've got all your new ID that identifies you as Nina Banks, but we've hit a snag and we're probably going to have to redo it all under a new name," Big Tag was saying. "Did you get the email I sent out?"

Nina sat in the conference room at McKay-Taggart. Unlike the London office, this one wasn't set in a gorgeous botanical BDSM club like The Garden. The Dallas office was sleek and modern, reminding her this was all business and she shouldn't be thinking about the gorgeous man next to her as anything but a client. JT Malone had shown up long before she'd thought he would, walking into the conference room with his twin, Michael. His identical twin, though it was easy to tell them apart. Michael was grave and serious, where JT's smile lit up the room.

She forced herself to focus on the authority figure. "Yes, sir. I got it this morning. I don't think it will be an issue and it won't require a new name. I think the best cover would be going in as Mr. Malone's friend. From what I understand, plus ones are perfectly acceptable at this retreat."

Charlotte Taggart sat next to her husband and a single brow rose over her intelligent eyes. "Really? I was going to go with journalist. You're a reporter writing a story about young business leaders and how they're shaking up Wall Street. I can put it out there that you've interviewed Andrew Lawless from 4L and a man named Seth Stark. They're both willing to back up the story if anyone asks."

That was an excellent cover. Truly bloody excellent, and she couldn't use it. And she couldn't tell Charlotte why she couldn't use it. What was she supposed to say now?

The silence lengthened, and Nina fought the urge to stand up and walk out. Her brain was blank. She was better than this. The man next to her was short-circuiting all her best instincts.

"That won't work." JT came to the rescue. "Everyone knows I don't talk to reporters. I've got a thing about it. Right, Mike?"

Michael Malone frowned and sat back, giving his brother what could only be described as the evil eye. "You've got a thing about sleeping with the wrong people. You see, my brother slept with the reporter who was supposedly doing a story on the family business. After he slept with her it turned into an exposé of how our family was disintegrating and wealth had ruined us all."

JT groaned. "I was twenty-two and I was upset because my brother had run off and joined the Navy and left me all alone. I get chatty when I have a couple of beers, and she used me. And I don't sleep with the wrong people anymore. I sleep with the right ones, even if they seem like they're the wrong ones."

She could feel every inch of her skin going pink, but she fought through it. "Mr. Malone knows his people best. I think we can come up with a good cover where I go in as his companion."

"Fiancée," JT corrected.

Now it was Big Tag's brow rising. "I don't think that's a good idea. Nina prefers keeping a polite distance in these kinds of operations. If she's your fiancée, she'll have to stay in the same room with you. Unless we're pretending like it's 1820 and Sandra is guarding her virginity. That might require a different wardrobe. How do you feel about turtlenecks?"

She should have told him the truth. Or at least some facsimile of it. She should have known nothing got past Big Tag. "I met with Mr. Malone earlier. We ran into each other at the hotel. Unfortunately, we also were accosted by several of the members of his leadership team who were there looking for answers about the senior Mr. Malone's illness. We were seen together, and Mr. Malone introduced me as his fiancée."

"I panicked." JT had the earnest thing down. "I'm sorry I put Ms. Blunt in this position, but honestly, it's for the best. I wouldn't bring a new girlfriend to this retreat."

"He's never brought a girlfriend at all," Michael admitted.

"I brought Dana," JT said quietly.

Michael turned his way, a sympathetic look crossing his face. "Dana wasn't your girlfriend. She was a friend. She was a girl."

Oh, now she very much wanted to know who Dana was. JT's jaw had tightened, his eyes going down.

"Well, she was the only friend I ever brought, so it would be odd for me to show up with someone I wasn't serious about. I've had a couple of girlfriends over the years and I didn't take them on the leadership family retreat because those girlfriends weren't family," JT replied, his voice perfectly even. "I'm not a spy, Mr. Taggart. I'm not good at this. I understand how to get oil out of the ground. That's about it. If I screwed this up, then maybe we should think about scrapping the whole thing. I know trust is important in this business."

"So is corporate espionage." The last member of their group seemed to peel away from the shadows. He was lanky, with gray eyes and pitch-black hair that tumbled over his forehead in a very boy-band way.

Nina stared at him and then back to Tag. "You've vetted him, right? You actually talked to someone at Langley and made sure he's not some operative's teenager who went a bit wild?"

Big Tag gave her a genuine smile. So often the man smirked in that arrogant way of his. "I assure you, he's the real deal. Mr. Magenta there is straight out of Langley. Gen Y is now in the house."

JT seemed relieved to get to talk about anything but the way they'd screwed up. Though she had to admit he'd done everything he could to take the heat off her. "He's the CIA guy? I thought he was like your kid or something."

"My oldest kids are in first grade," Tag said, his brows furrowing. "He's at least a freshman."

The young operative put his hands on his hips. "I'm twenty-three, asshole. And I'm not Mr. Magenta. I asked you to call me Mr. Black."

"No can do. I already killed Mr. Black," Tag shot back. "Blew his ass all over the Arabian Sea."

Charlotte stared his way.

Tag put a hand over his wife's. "No, baby. We share everything. Including our successes. I shared the unholy amount of money you brought into this marriage, all the children, and I share in your kills, too." He slid a slow smile her way. "I'll give you half the credit when I track down Levi Green and stuff his entrails so far up his ass they come out his nose."

Charlotte appeared perfectly fine with that. "Deal, baby." She turned back to the CIA employee. "And I think Mr. Magenta suits you. Your generation is very gender fluid. I applaud that heartily."

The kid was staring at Tag in apparent horror. "You do know what entrails are, right? They're kind of already attached to the ass."

"Not after I get done with them, they're not." Tag started to explain his version of revenge in ridiculously over-the-top detail.

"Is this that thing where CIA agents don't want you to know their real names, so they make one up?" JT leaned her way, his voice going low. "I've only met two in my time and they both called themselves Mr. Black."

She turned slightly so she could whisper his way. "Sometimes an operative will go under a different name to keep anonymity. Mr. Black or Mrs. White or something like that. Why did you deal with the Agency?"

"I drill in some of the world's hot spots," he replied. "Trust me. I've met with Agency reps. I was working in the Middle East and they contacted me about putting a man named John Brown on the payroll so it looked like he had a job there. He's still on Malone Oil employment files. Then there was a lady named Jane White who needed access to a conference we were attending."

Michael leaned over while Tag and the Agency kid were arguing about murdering a CIA asset. "Did you sleep with her?"

Michael knew?

JT sent his brother a nasty look. "I did not."

"Fine, call me Drake." The kid sank down into his chair.

Tag actually gagged. "No. I will not call you Drake. Where did you get that name? From a bad soap opera?"

"From my mother, asshole," the kid replied. "You know I might be young, but I'm a freaking genius, and I'm creative. I'm also really good with all the latest poisons. I won't kill you, but I will make your dick shrivel up. Would you like a cup of coffee, man?"

Charlotte laughed. "Oh, you'll do well, Drake. And I'm sorry, but go for it. I had our fourth kid recently, so I'm okay with not seeing his dick again."

Big Tag was grinning. "Don't be so quick to act on that. I'm going to get my balls scooped out and then we can play forever." He turned to the kid. "Drake it is then. Drake, I know we've read the pertinent reports, but I would like for you to go over it all again since our primary has changed. According to his brother, JT is a himbo who doesn't read much."

JT sent his brother his middle finger.

It made her think about the fact that her sister had always casually tossed her under any bus she could. Alicia was petite and perfect, super feminine, and far more interested in her hair than her studies. She understood how JT must feel.

"I believe Mr. Malone understands the operation well enough," she said. "He certainly understands his business, and the technology they're trying to steal was something he helped develop, so how about we don't disparage his intellect."

That had every head in the room turning her way, but she wasn't about to back down. It might be time to remember that she was a badass and he was her partner.

For now.

Tag gave her a nod. "All right. Drake…that's so bad." His wife's hand came out, slapping against his chest, and he seemed to take her cue. "Please go over what you've found and why we're doing this."

"I would definitely like to know why you think my admin is a spy," JT said. "She's a major bitch, and I actually say that with respect. She's smart and she takes absolutely no shit off anyone, which given that she's a female in the petroleum industry, she kind of has to. And no, I've never slept with her."

"Not because she hasn't tried," Michael said under his breath.

Well, that cleared up a few things. She needed to treat JT like he was any other partner she was going to go into an op with. Especially one who didn't have training and was absolutely above reproach. JT wasn't trying to sell his own tech. He was a man who'd been thrown into something he wasn't ready for.

He was a man who wouldn't understand how badly this could go because there was a core of goodness to JT Malone that wouldn't allow him to see that dark side. He was shoved into a world where everything and everyone had two faces.

"I believe the team discovered a connection between a few of the suspects," she said. "I can go over the whole report with you later, but a man named Greg Hutchins has been working with Mr. Drake here."

"Just Drake," the CIA agent corrected. "And yes, I've been working with Hutch."

"I know him. He's a good guy," JT said.

"Where do you know Hutch from?" She was curious. According to everything she knew, David Malone was their primary contact with Malone Oil. The Dallas office provided the company's security here in the States, while they worked with former CIA agent Tennessee Smith in the more remote locations of the world. But as far as she knew, Malone Oil had in-house cybersecurity, which was Hutch's specialty.

"I know him from the club," JT replied.

"The club?"

"Sanctum."

The room seemed to get much, much hotter. He was a member of Sanctum? He belonged to a damn BDSM club? He would be a Dom, an indulgent one. He would be the kind of top she'd always dreamed of.

"Of course," she replied, praying her voice hadn't gone up a notch.

"Hutch hasn't spent any time at Malone Oil," Big Tag explained. "He's done some consulting with their IT department, but they don't know what he looks like. It's why he's on a plane right now. He's going in as the resort's IT guy, but don't think he can't handle himself. Like Sandra, he's there to back you up if you need it."

"He's a very smart guy. I don't understand why he left the Agency." Drake looked thoughtful for a moment. "He could have gone places."

Hutch had been one of Ten's men, as her boss Damon Knight referred to them. Michael had been on Ten's team as well.

Michael leaned forward, giving the CIA agent his attention. "I left at the same time. We didn't like how the Agency treated our boss."

Drake shrugged one broad shoulder. "You were on a Special Ops team. You were good cannon fodder. Hutch was on track to be an agent."

JT snorted slightly. "Well, I'm sure you were the best cannon fodder, Mike. Now someone tell me who you think stole my prototype. I've been working on that material for years. I was worried it was my chief engineer."

"Your chief engineer is dead," Tag said flatly.

"Yeah, he was in a car..." JT stopped. "You think someone killed him. You thought he was the one, didn't you?"

"Yes," Drake acknowledged. "We discovered William Murphy was meeting with a man we believe works for the Reconnaissance General Bureau."

Nina leaned toward JT because the only reason she knew what Drake was talking about was years of intelligence work. "North Korean spy agency."

He gave her the most intimate smile. "Thanks."

She was not going to go gooey. "But we'll be looking for a Westerner. His name is Joe Hall. He formerly worked for the embassy in South Korea, which is where the North Koreans likely recruited him. He's the go-between. He's the one who met with your engineer."

JT shook his head. "Bill and I worked together for years. Why would he do this?"

Charlotte took that question. "He was diagnosed with terminal cancer six months ago. I believe he was looking for a payout to help his family."

The expression on JT's face made her heart twist. "He didn't tell me. He's got two kids and his wife…she quit her job to stay home with them. I went to his funeral and they didn't say anything."

"Probably because I could arrest the wife if I could prove she was involved in his decision," Drake mused. "I haven't been able to yet."

"Leave her alone." JT pointed his way. "She's going through enough. You leave her out of this."

Mike put a hand on his brother's shoulder. "Hey, I'm sorry about Bill. I know he was a friend of yours, but he was spying."

"No, he was in a bad place and didn't know how to get out of it." JT sat back, looking weary. "I should have known."

"He should have told you, but he didn't, and we'll leave his wife out of it. Somehow I don't think a housewife from Houston will be doing any spy work," Tag offered. "Now the reason we believe one of the workers on this retreat killed him is the fact that they all had contact with the engineer in his final days."

"We have an office in Houston," JT explained. "He worked out of there. I would expect a lot of people came in contact with him."

Drake was studying JT as though trying to figure him out. "But only three of them are going to the retreat." He pulled a tablet out of his bag and flipped it around to show JT something. "Your assistant took a vacation to Hawaii a few weeks ago."

It was a screen capture of one of Deanna's social media pages. She was wearing a bikini, a fruity drink in her hand, with the caption "loving life in Oahu."

JT nodded. "Yeah, she takes two weeks a year and almost always goes to Hawaii. I'm afraid my business isn't great for fun travel. We're in the Middle East a lot. And North Dakota. It's not so surprising she's goes to the islands with her friends. Friend. From what I can tell she's only got the one."

"There's a problem with this picture." Drake moved his finger over the screen to zero in on the sign behind her. *The Beach Bar, established 1972.* "The Beach Bar burned down six months before she posted this shot. All the other shots of her vacation appear to be from different times as well. Except for this one."

He switched the picture to one of a plate of sushi with the caption "time for dinner."

"I would think sushi is pretty popular in Hawaii." There was a frown on JT's face, like he knew something bad was coming but he didn't want to hear it.

"I tracked down the plates and the presentation of the sushi along with the silverware and flatware and table linen. There's only one restaurant that has all of those in combination and that's Harold's," Drake explained.

Drake was a desktop investigator. She would bet he'd been recruited for his hacking skills, or he'd designed some software the Agency was interested in. She would also bet all of his experience was technical, which was exactly why Big Tag was sending in Sandra and Hutch—both military vets. But the kid was good.

JT sighed. "Harold's is in Houston."

"And the particular sushi she's eating was a special from a night two days before your engineer died and the prototype went missing," Drake explained.

"There's a reason I stay off social media," Big Tag said with a shake of his head.

"And the rest?" JT asked.

It was easy to see that this whole discussion was bothering JT. She wasn't sure what to do about it. "According to the reports I've read, the other two were in Houston that week for a conference. The truth is all you need to worry about is giving me cover. I'll handle the mission once we get to the island. I assume Mr. Drake will be coming with us."

"I will," Drake acknowledged. "Because the whole resort has been bought out by Malone Oil, my only choice is to go in as staff. I'll be working as waitstaff. Hutch assures me we'll be able to have eyes on the suspects at all times. I believe the North Korean asset will likely try to make the drop someplace outside the resort. You have a few activities planned off site, correct?"

"We have deep-sea fishing one day, and there's a beach on the other side of the island where we'll go for a picnic. There's also hiking pretty much every day. It's not hard to get away from the group," JT admitted.

Tag pointed his way. "That's why we'll need everyone to take shifts. I would like to have Nina in a less high-profile position, but it seems like that option isn't on the table."

She didn't think JT needed more guilt. The poor man had been through a lot this morning. He'd found out his one-night stand was going to turn into a week-long nightmare, and that people he'd trusted had betrayed him. She knew what that felt like all too well. "I can make it work. I can certainly keep an eye on the admin. Or rather, she'll keep an eye on me since she's already accused me of being a hooker."

Big Tag looked right at Drake. "A hooker is a woman who sells her sexual services for cash. Although some might take credit cards now."

Drake's eyes rolled so far back Nina was almost certain he could see inside his own brain.

"And we should call them sex workers," Charlotte added.

"That's what I thought, too." It was good to know they were on the same page. Girl power. "She seemed very rude."

"She is. You'll have a time with that one," Michael said. "I've never understood why JT didn't fire her."

JT pushed back off the table and stood. "Is that all? Because Nina and I should probably get to work. What's your wardrobe like?"

"It's like clothing. Normal amount of cotton blends. I brought a nice pair of trainers," she admitted.

JT shook his head. "We're going shopping. You're supposed to be the fiancée of a billionaire. I assure you Deanna will know exactly how much your clothes and shoes cost. We've got a week until we go to the island. I have to do some work at the office, but with my father being sick, they can't expect me in every day. However, I'm going to assume it might help for them to see you coming up to the office to spend some time with me. You'll need to be dressed properly, and by properly I mean expensively."

Charlotte sighed. "I like the makeover part best."

Makeover? But he did have a point. Her clothes were perfectly fine for an assistant coming to her first retreat. Not so great for a coddled and indulged fiancée.

"I think you two should spend a lot of time together between now and the retreat," Big Tag announced. "You need to get your stories straight. I mean it. I want you to speak in one voice when someone asks you how you met. You need to figure it all out right down to where you proposed. One person is already dead. I'm not going to lose Damon's newest operative because of chemistry."

"Our chemistry is…" she began.

JT put a hand on her arm. "Of course. We'll work on that this afternoon. Maybe I can make her like me by buying a shit ton of expensive shoes."

Charlotte sighed. "It always works for me. Go to Nordstrom and ask for Helena."

"We've put three of Helena's children through private school with Charlie's purchases." Big Tag stood and gave his lady a hand up. "Come on, baby. I can hear Travis from here."

Sure enough, a low wail was coming from the hallway. Charlotte Taggart had recently given birth to her fourth child, a son they'd named Travis Taggart. There was a daycare on this floor, so the employees didn't have to be far from their children. Damon was talking about expanding the nursery they kept at The Garden for Oliver Knight and Nathan Carter. When Hayley went back to work, her and Nick's daughter would be joining the boys.

She liked the daycare, liked having the children close.

"Mrs. Taggart, he woke up hungry." A young woman strode in carrying a tiny bundle in her arms.

"He's always hungry." Big Tag held out his arms and took the baby. "Come on, son. Let's go to my office. I'm not going to miss a chance to see your mom's boobs. Now remember, you're only renting. I bought."

Charlotte laughed as she followed them. "Have fun. I'll expect all the *Pretty Woman*-like details the next time we talk."

"Yeah, I suspect we'll definitely have a talk very soon." Michael was watching his brother like he didn't want to let him go.

But she rather thought JT'd had enough of his brother's opinions for one day. She reached for his hand. "We should probably get used to showing each other some affection in public."

His fingers immediately tangled with hers, sliding in like they were puzzle pieces. "Yeah, we should. I'm known for being pretty affectionate with my girlfriends."

"You are?" Michael's brow had risen.

He squeezed her hand. "I am. You're not around much so you wouldn't know. Come on, baby. I'm going to call you baby."

It's what he'd called her the night before when he'd held on to her so tight she thought he would never let go. Just the word coming out of that man's mouth sent a shiver of desire through her.

"Ms. Blunt, could I have a moment of your time?" Drake asked.

JT took a step back, and she hated that she felt colder without his hand in hers. "I'll go pull my truck around. I'll meet you out front."

Michael followed his brother and she was left alone with the CIA agent.

"I know I'm young, but don't underestimate me." There was a hint of steel in Drake's gaze. "This is my op. I don't care what Taggart says. If I'd had my way, I wouldn't have called any of you in, but Malone wouldn't work with an Agency team."

"Good for Malone."

"I have to wonder about that. Given that his son used to be on an Agency team, I would have assumed he understood, but we all make do with what we have, I suppose. I checked into you."

She stood up a little straighter. "I would expect nothing less."

"I read about the situation that led to you leaving Interpol. I will assume you've learned from your mistakes."

"I hope so. If you have a real problem with me, I can get on a plane back to England this evening." It might be for the best. But she also hated the idea of JT going in alone. He was obviously out of his depths, and one person had already been killed over that prototype. JT wanted to believe in his people, and he would need someone to look out for him.

It had nothing to do with the fact that she could feel his hands on her body.

"Not at all." Drake was roughly six foot four, with a muscular build that hadn't completely filled out yet. "I prefer to work with experienced agents, and there's no better experience than failure. At least that's what everyone tells me. I think a woman who's been burned before likely will play a relationship cover with care. She won't get caught up in a handsome face and miss the clues."

"Clues?"

"JT Malone was in Houston, too," Drake pointed out. "JT Malone is the only one I know of with the mechanical expertise to have done the job on the engineer's car. It was quite a professional job. I doubt the admin would know how to do more than hook up her smart phone."

"Why would JT do something like this? It's his company."

"And he feels trapped. He blames his brother for leaving him behind. I've made a study of the man," Drake stated. "I believe this could be some revenge on his part. This would be the ultimate betrayal of his brother's beliefs."

"Do you have any family?" Despite the fact that he was an operative and obviously brilliant, he was still only twenty-three. She had to treat him like the young adult he was, and that meant educating him when he needed it.

"No. I'm an only child."

"Then you can read all you like about JT Malone, but you can't understand him in this. I can. I have a younger sister. She's horrible. I mean she's the worst human being on the face of the planet. And if someone tried to hurt her, I would stand in their way. Because I am her older sister. Because it's what we do. She's awful to me in social situations and yet when everything went down with Interpol, she was there for me. She's the one who found Damon Knight and pushed me to interview. What you witnessed here today was irritation. Nothing more."

"I'm going to ask you to keep an open mind and open eyes," Drake said.

"Always." But she didn't believe for a second that JT had anything to do with the theft and espionage. The kid might know how to figure out a mystery, but he couldn't read people yet.

"And it's obvious Mr. Malone is trying to charm you. I suggest you keep a cautious distance." Drake's eyes came up. "If you find yourself needing company, give me a call."

She stared at him for a moment. "Are you seriously telling me to call you if I get horny, little boy?"

The right side of his mouth kicked up in a grin that made her think one day the kid might have some game. "Spying is a stressful business, Nina."

She turned and walked away. It was going to be a long op.

* * * *

JT ignored the buzzing of his cell. He knew exactly who it was, and he did not want to talk to his brother right now.

He was going to have a hard enough time talking to Nina, since he was almost completely certain she was going to try to pull away.

He wasn't going to let her. He was going to have one good damn thing come out of all of this, and it would be getting a chance with that British honey.

Oh, and she had tasted sweet. He should have had most of the morning to get his mouth on her again, but no. Someone had to be an asshole.

Someone had to be a traitor.

There was a knock on the window and there she was. He unlocked the door and she slid in beside him.

"We should talk."

"Of course." He pulled out onto Pearl Street. He'd known she was going to want to talk about how everything had gone sideways, but that wasn't where he was going to lead the conversation. He liked to keep things positive. After all, that was how he dealt with almost everything. "First off, you're going to need at least three bikinis. I think you'll look gorgeous in blue. It will totally distract the bad guys."

"I didn't mean we should talk about what I'm going to wear, JT. I mean we need to talk about the fact that we didn't know we were going to work together when we slept together."

He wasn't going to argue with her about that. "Well, now we know we're totally compatible. It probably would have been awkward if we'd been thrown together and told 'hey, now you're engaged.'"

She sent him an adorably irritated frown. "Well, for one thing we wouldn't have to pretend to be engaged if your employees hadn't caught me in your bedroom. And why did you go straight for engaged?"

"I thought it was easier than saying we'd actually gotten married." He snapped his fingers as he remembered something. "We should stop by Tiffany and get you a ring. At least three carats."

Her eyes went gorgeously wide. "Three carats? As in diamond?"

"Of course," he replied. "Unless you'd rather have a sapphire. It's up to you. Anything you want. But I'm serious about the blue bikini. Also, you'll need at least three cocktail dresses. It's not too formal, but the women do tend to dress up."

She shook her head as though forcing herself to focus. "I don't need an engagement ring."

"You do. Look, I'm fully willing to leave all the spy stuff to you, and you leave all the fancy stuff to me. I know I look like I rode in off the range, but I have excellent taste. I get that from my mother. She's British, too. Why she married my ornery old dad I have no idea. My momma is a lady of the highest order, and she taught me to appreciate the finer things in life." He needed her unfocused, or rather focused on him. "See, we can start a new tradition. In this relationship, the women shoot and the men make things pretty. Don't discount making things pretty. I've spent months at a time on oil rigs, and I would have killed for some decorative pillows."

"I don't want to talk about clothes or jewelry," she insisted, though there was a huff in her breath that told him she kind of did want to, but she was going to be all business. "Obviously you know best how to help me fit in with your people. We need to talk about the fact that we slept together and now we're going on an op."

That was a perfect setup. "And sharing a room, so again, I think we've made things far less awkward. You will like our room. It's the presidential suite."

"Does it have separate bedrooms?" She asked the question like the right answer could solve all her problems.

"They can connect several rooms when the resort isn't full, but Dad likes to keep everyone close, so we're all in one wing of the resort." She wasn't getting away that easily. He stopped at the red light and turned her way. "Are you saying you don't want to sleep with me? Did I snore?"

"No." Her face fell.

Oh, this was exactly how to deal with the gorgeous operative. She might be good at killing the bad guys, but she didn't want to break his heart. He'd noticed her compassion while they'd been in the meeting earlier. She hadn't liked it when Mike had put him in a bad position. She was a woman who picked sides and was inherently loyal. He knew exactly how to work her. "Was it…was it bad for you?"

She groaned and her head fell back. "It was fabulous and you know it."

He did. He gave her a grin. He knew he was being a manipulative bastard, but he fought for what he wanted, and he wanted her. "It was good for me, too. It was kind of the best."

She'd gone a delicious shade of pink. "Really?"

"Really." He turned onto the access road. It was good to be alone with her again. The conference had unnerved him. His brother constantly said he was naïve, and now he might have to agree with him since it appeared someone had been murdered on his watch. "It was one of the best nights of my life. Followed by one of the hardest afternoons."

Her hand came out, covering his own. "I know it was rough. You need to remember that none of this is your fault."

It was difficult to think that way. He was the boss. His dad might walk into the office and everyone bowed down, but he'd left the day-to-day operations to JT for the last few years. His father was getting ready to retire. "It doesn't feel that way. I should have seen that something was going on with Bill. I need to figure out how to take care of his family without making his wife uncomfortable. Bill's wife is very proud. Not in a snooty way, but she's not one to take handouts, which is why I would be shocked if she knew what Bill was doing. He was desperate. I can't imagine what that must feel like."

Nina was staring at him, a sheen of tears in her eyes. "There aren't many people in the world who could find out an employee committed an act of sabotage and still find a way to care about him."

He put his eyes on the road. "I believe my twin would say I'm naïve and inexperienced."

"Is he right? Have you been sheltered all your life?"

"Sheltered from certain things, yes. I've never had to worry about money, so I don't think much of it. But I've been out in the world. In my brother's eyes, because I've never been a part of a military unit, I'm soft. He's never been on an oil rig when pirates decide to show up. They're real, you know."

"I do," she replied quietly. "They're troublesome and violent."

"And I was in charge of that rig. I'm in charge wherever I go." He could still remember how scared he'd been that he would lose his workers. He was responsible for their safety. "Did I want to shoot the fuckers? Hell, yeah, I did. But I had to sit there and negotiate because we were outgunned."

"That was the smart thing to do," Nina assured him. "You took care of your people."

And then he'd worked with some locals to take the pirates down. "I've had to deal with mobsters, and I didn't speak their language. I didn't have a team of badasses behind me. I had engineers and geologists. I've also seen some of the worst poverty in the world and known that everything I have would be a drop in the well of trying to cure it. But I can help Bill's family. I can make a difference to them."

"You could always tell her the company took out an insurance policy on him because he was so important and replacing him would have been costly," she suggested. "It was an outdated policy from years ago. But now you realize that money should go to them."

She was good at this. He wasn't the only one who could manipulate his way around a situation. "That could work. She shouldn't have to worry about her future when she's in mourning. I'll put that into play. Thanks, baby."

Her shoulders went straight. "You can't call me baby."

He had an answer to her denial. "I thought I was supposed to call you that. You're really more of a baby than a sweetheart. My dad calls my mom honey, so that doesn't work. Not that you aren't sweet."

She shook her head, obviously flustered again. "See, that's what we can't do."

"I thought that was what I was supposed to do. We're getting married."

"We're getting fake married." She thought about that for a second. "No, we're fake engaged. We're not actually getting fake married."

"You're going to leave me at the fake altar?"

"There is no altar. Fake or otherwise."

"All right. You want a non-conventional fake wedding. I can make that happen."

A frustrated groan came from the back of her throat. "JT, we have to work together."

He smiled her way. "I know. I think we're going to be good at it. I feel way better knowing you're going in with me. Though we should talk about a couple of things. You know about Sanctum, right? It's a lifestyle club."

"I work in a lifestyle club."

He'd been curious about this part of her life. "Are you in the lifestyle? I have Master rights at Sanctum."

"I have Master rights at The Garden," she replied.

He knew damn well that was a lie, and he wished he had the right to spank her pretty ass. "No you don't, sub."

She kept her eyes on the road, but there was some humor in her tone. "How do you know I'm not a top?"

"Because I topped you last night. I took control and you responded beautifully." Knowing that she was in the lifestyle actually explained a few things to him. She had responded when he'd taken control, and she likely would enjoy more dominance when it came to the bedroom.

"What if I told you I was a switch?"

He wouldn't have guessed she would like to ever top anyone during sex, but he could give it a go. After all, being a top was all about giving a bottom what they needed. "I would ask if you needed a real sub to top or if I could learn how to do that for you because I think I would have trouble watching you with someone else."

She was quiet for a moment. "Are you for real?"

"Last time I checked." He drove in silence for a moment, trying to figure out how she was feeling. "I'm not perfect. Far from it."

"From where I'm sitting you're pretty close." She shifted in her seat. "So we should talk about how this needs to go."

"Yes. I think we should start with some minor impact play." He wasn't going to have this conversation with her. Not the one about all the reasons they shouldn't continue to sleep together. There wasn't any reason they should stop. In fact, it would help their cover if they were sleeping together. She was clinging to some rule that didn't need to apply to them.

"I take back the part where I said you're perfect. You're obviously very thick."

He could turn that around, too. "I'm glad you noticed. I thought it worked well lengthwise, too."

She stared at him. "You think I'm talking about your dick, don't you?"

He did not in any way think she'd been talking about his cock, but he'd learned that hiding his intelligence could help him out in numerous ways. It was always good to be underestimated. "And I appreciate the compliment. Now let's talk lingerie because there's always some asshole who shows up in the early morning hours and I can't have them thinking I force you to wear my old shirts. They'll start to worry about my finances, and then they talk to a reporter and suddenly my stock tanks. I think there's a La Perla here."

"La Perla?" She sat up straight, smoothing back her hair. "You're not going to be serious about this, are you?"

"I'm perfectly serious about giving you the best cover possible."

"It's not going to work," she said quietly.

"Yeah, it will." He was talking about exactly what she was. It would work. They could work. But she wasn't ready to hear that yet.

Nina went stiff, and for a moment he was worried she was going to insist they have this fight here and now. That was something he wasn't ready for. Not even close. "JT, do you see the SUV behind us?"

He glanced in the rearview mirror. Sure enough, there was a gray SUV behind them, a single male in the driver's seat. "Yes."

"Take the next exit. I want to see if he follows."

He did as she asked, getting off of 75 and turning left on Mockingbird. The SUV followed close behind. "What do you want me to do?"

"Let's stop and have some lunch and see if he picks up after we're done. I'll send Big Tag the plate number just in case." She was on her phone, texting. "I could use some Mexican. It's the one thing I can't get in London. I mean, obviously we have Mexican restaurants, but it's not the same."

Mexican it was then. And then he would show her exactly what he had to offer her.

# Chapter Five

Nina stood in the middle of the private dressing room that had to be meant for large bridal parties since it was the size of a small house and had two chaise lounges available for customers. She'd already been offered champagne—which she'd forced herself to turn down.

This was JT's world. Not hers. It couldn't be hers.

How had that man stayed so sweetly down to earth when he obviously lived in heaven?

She forced herself back to the problems at hand.

Someone was following them, and that meant she couldn't have the conversation they needed to have. Not that he would let them have it since he seemed to deliberately misunderstand everything she said.

"I brought five cocktail dresses for you to try on." The salesperson strode into the room. She was perfectly dressed, a testament to her dedication to her job, which was to make sure everyone who walked in the door looked good. And expensive.

The salesperson hung the dresses on the rack of the private dressing room they'd been shown to after they'd torn through the shoe section. Charlotte had been right. Helena knew her shoes. She now had the most spectacular pair of sexed-up Louboutins she'd ever seen. JT hadn't let her stop there. She had ten new pairs. Apparently her sad pair of flip-flops wouldn't do for pool time. She'd required Valentino studded sandals in three different colors.

She didn't even want to think about the fact that he wanted to take her to Tiffany after this and buy her a ring that would likely require its own security detail.

Not her. Fake fiancée her.

She would pay him back for the clothes, but they would be returning that ring.

"Let me know if you need anything." The salesperson stopped at the door, her voice going low. "Just so you know, your man is the sweetest thing. He told us to bring you anything you wish and to treat you like you're the most important person in the world. Because that's what you are to him. So sweet."

Yep, he was a charmer. He was sweet and gorgeous and rich as sin. He seemed to genuinely care about the people around him, and he was thick in both head and cock.

"He's the best." She shut the door and took a deep breath.

He was definitely the best at making her crazy. He'd been beyond attentive. He'd held her hand at lunch, his thumb stroking the pulse point on her wrist, making her go all soft and gooey. He'd claimed they should do it because their stalker might be watching.

He made her wish this was something more than cover for an op.

*Why can't it be? It's obvious he's into you. You're crazy about him. Why not let yourself try again? Yes, you made a mistake with Roger, but that doesn't mean you punish yourself forever. JT isn't Roger. He wouldn't lie to you.*

She barely knew the man, but she was already certain he would never lie to her. Maybe she was the naïve one.

Her mobile buzzed and she looked down at a text from Big Tag.

*Your stalker is a pro. PI named Howard Benson. Someone's looking into you. We've had hits all over on your cover. Expect that he's got eyes on you. Fun fact—he's worked for Malone Oil before, so ask your new boy toy if he's told the parents the happy news. Congrats on your fake engagement. Try not to get fake pregnant.*

Damn it. She would bet on the admin. It hadn't taken her long to start looking into the new girl. The question became was Deanna protecting her boss or her own turf? It would make a big difference in how she handled the woman.

She needed to pick a couple of dresses and get back to the office. The office would be an excellent place to hide from JT. She might even be able to hole up in one of the offices and get some advice from the ladies on how to lose a guy she really, really didn't want to lose.

Of course, if she went back to the office, the PI would know something was up. It made perfect sense to go there once. Her fake fiancée's brother worked there. They could play it off that way. But spending hours up there on her own would be suspicious.

Things had gotten much more complex. No one would have thought about David Malone's assistant. She would have been one more worker.

As JT's fiancée, she would be center stage.

Should she pull out?

"You doing okay in there?" JT's deep voice came through the door of the dressing room.

"It depends," she whispered. "Do you know a man named Howard Benson?"

"The private investigator?"

She opened the door because this was a conversation they needed to have very quietly. "Yes. Why do you need an outside private investigator? You have a whole firm of them."

He walked in and closed the door behind him. "I didn't hire him. Deanna did during her divorce. She didn't want to use McKay-Taggart because they're damn expensive. I offered to help pay for it, but she can be stubborn. She thought her husband was cheating. He was. On her and his girlfriend."

Well, at least she knew who'd hired the PI and why Deanna was so touchy. "He's the man following us. Are you sure your relationship with this woman is strictly professional?"

His eyes had gone innocently wide. "I've never touched her. Not once. I don't think I've ever even helped her out of a car."

She stared at him.

"I'm serious. Never touched her. Never been anything but professional with her. She's abrupt but effective," he explained.

"She's rude."

"She's direct. I wanted to fire her in the beginning and my dad took me aside and asked me why. I told him she was abrasive. He asked me if I would say the same thing about a man in her position. I gave her more time and looked at her differently. She's good at her job. I don't care that she's not what a female assistant is supposed to be. If I asked her to get my coffee there would likely be poison in it, but if I direct her to push through a multimillion-dollar deal with a jackhole who's trying to tie me up in red tape, she gets it done. I can get my own coffee." He seemed to deflate. "All that said, she did seem jealous today."

She'd seemed more than jealous. "I think we can assume she set the PI on us. Have you talked to your parents? Would she call and ask about me?"

"Turn around."

"Why?"

"Because you still need to buy swimsuits," he said. "Let me help you try these on."

She sent him a pointed look.

"I've already seen everything, and we should talk about this in private in case the PI is lurking."

He was right. And he had seen everything. She turned and let him deal with the zipper she always struggled with. "Fine. Talk."

She could see him through the mirrors. All three of them. She watched as he smoothed his hands across her shoulders before he slowly eased the zipper down.

"I called my mom earlier today," he said. "She's been sent a bunch of information about you and how we met. She and my father will support the cover. If they get reporters calling, they'll hold the family line of 'we do not discuss our personal lives in the press.' They'll move on very quickly because there are far more interesting people out there with even more money. We're boring."

His fingers skimmed along her skin, making her shiver. "Good. I think it's safe to say Michael is on board as well. Are the two of you okay?"

"Can I kiss you? I have the wildest urge to put my lips on the back of your neck."

She wanted that more than anything. "It would be a mistake."

He touched a place between her shoulders that made her want to melt. "What you're telling me is I can do this job, or I can have you? Is that what this is about?"

She was going to have to live up to her name and be blunt with him. "I don't fuck where I work. I learned that the hard way. And you're avoiding the question. I asked about your brother."

"You're avoiding my question." He parted the dress, exposing her back. "Were you going to dump me this morning?"

It took everything she had to not lean back into him, offering her skin up for his touch. "Dumping you implies we had a relationship to begin with."

"I thought we made a connection. Was I wrong? If you can tell me you didn't feel anything last night, I'll figure out a way to make this thing work. I'll sleep on the floor if I need to."

She wanted to tell him that no, she hadn't felt anything, but it would be a lie. "Fine. I was going to ask you if we could see each other when I got back."

"Then let me kiss you."

"I told you I don't sleep with coworkers."

"Nina, baby, we're not coworkers. I'm the guy you're going to try to keep in line while you work. I'm your cover, not your partner. Once this job is over, we won't ever have to work together again. Not in this way because I fully intend to stay away from all the spy stuff." He went to the rack and pulled the emerald green cocktail dress off. "I think this one first."

Yes, he would pick that one. It had the lowest neckline. She took the dress from him and slipped it on. "I had a relationship with a coworker that went bad. I can't have another job go wrong because I was too busy thinking about a guy."

"You won't have to think about anything but getting the job done. I'll handle everything else," he promised. "That looks beautiful on you. Can I ask you a question?"

She looked in the mirror and had to admit the dress looked good on her. "You don't seem to have a problem with those."

"Do you want to see me again? Or has the day we've had shown you a different side of me? A side you don't like."

She turned, the dress forgotten. "No. I do want to see you, but I can't afford for this job to go sideways because we have feelings for each other. So I think we should wait to move anything forward. Maybe once we get on the other side of this job, we can reevaluate."

He got into her space, forcing her to look up at him. "It's too late. At least it is for me. I've already got feelings for you, and that's not going to change even if you tell me I can't kiss you again."

He was so close. So gorgeous. He was her every fantasy and he was standing right in front of her. Was she really going to let him go because of something Roger had done? "I should think about this. Introducing sex will merely complicate things."

"Sex has already been introduced. And now that I know you're a sub, I won't be able to think about anything else."

"I didn't tell you I was a sub." She'd tried to avoid that whole line of conversation because he'd been right. He had basically topped her the night before, and it had been fabulous. What would it be like if they could be a formal D/s couple?

"You didn't have to tell me." Every word came out of his mouth on a silky glide of his tongue. "I knew you were sexually submissive because of the way you melted for me. I didn't know you were an experienced sub, but I knew damn straight I could give you what you need."

"What do I need?" It wasn't his money. It wasn't his family.

"You need a man who lets you be the badass you are in your everyday life, and who helps you let it all go at night. You need a man who supports you in everything you want, including being his dirty little sex toy every night you're in the mood. Let me kiss you."

She'd promised herself this wouldn't happen again. Not until they weren't working together. "It's going to make things harder."

"I can't get harder, baby." His hands molded to her hips, his lips hovering over hers. "And I know you weren't talking about my cock. You think it will be harder to manage the mission, but we're going to be side by side every single day and every night. Do you really think we can stay away from each other?"

"We have to. Once we get there, I have to concentrate on the job."

"Not every minute of the day. That's why you have backup. No one can keep that kind of concentration up. You will need to relax." He loomed over her. "That's where I come in."

His words were hypnotic, almost as mesmerizing as his presence. "You'll help me relax?"

He was staring at her like she was something precious, like he couldn't take his eyes off her. "I'll play things any way you want when you're working, but you get a couple of hours a day when I'm in charge. Of course, you know you're still in charge deep down, but during that time, my goal will be to get you out of your head, to force you to let go of all the stress that comes with being the person you are. Strong. Brave. In control."

It was everything she'd ever wanted. "And what do you get out of it?"

"I get to concentrate on you," he said. "I get to let go of everything that makes me tense and crazy and focus on something that makes me happy. You."

He was too much. How was she supposed to believe him? Or should she go with the fantasy of him since in two weeks she would be back in London? What could it truly hurt to sleep with him for a couple of nights? Staying close to him was good for their cover, and if she was in the same room with him, why shouldn't they touch each other?

"I'm not getting serious about you," she explained. "My life is in London." What there was of it. "I'm going to be here for a few weeks and then I'll be back home."

Back to real life, which didn't include a hot cowboy god of a Dom.

She would be back to watching all her friends have kids and settle down, to worrying about her friends who were in trouble and didn't want to be found.

A slow smile spread across his face, like he knew he'd won the battle. "I might make you want to stay."

She shook her head. Like she'd thought before, he was too much. She would fall so hard for him, and it would disintegrate at some point in time. She couldn't handle it again. "I won't. I'll get on a plane to London and I'll go back to my world. But maybe a few weeks in yours wouldn't be terrible."

"It wouldn't be terrible at all," he said, his fingers tangling in her hair. His eyes suddenly went hard, but in an incredibly sexy "I'm taking charge" way. "I think you should relax right now."

There were reasons for her to not do that at the moment. "We've got a PI looking for us."

"And if he shows up, what will he find, Nina? Will he find us plotting how to bring down a spy, or will he find us doing what engaged couples most like to engage in?"

The man knew how to make sense, but he was forgetting a few things. "And the saleslady?"

"Will be happy to let me stay in here for the rest of the day because she's smart and she knows I'm going to tell her we'll take it all at the end of this." Those fingers tightened, pulling at her scalp in a perfectly delicious way. "Do you agree that I'm in charge when it's time to relax?"

She could fight him, but she didn't want to. Not in any way. She knew she was bargaining but she couldn't help herself. Perhaps if she went into the relationship knowing it wouldn't last, she wouldn't get hurt in the end. "You're in charge."

"Damn straight I am. Now turn around."

"Am I going to try anything else on?"

"I told you we'll take them all. As for trying something on, yeah, you're going to try me on. I think I'll fit just fine."

Her whole body lit up at the dark tone his voice had taken. He'd used a form of this tone the night before, but this time he'd deepened his voice. Maybe it was unconscious, but it was obvious he'd gone into top space, and that made her skin sing in anticipation. She turned and he had the dress off her, allowing her to step out of it before he laid it on the bench. Then he had the clasp of her bra undone in a heartbeat. He tossed it aside, and that was when she noticed she could see herself in the mirror ahead. She wore nothing but the pair of white cotton undies she'd put on earlier in the day.

"You're so fucking pretty," he said, his hands winding around her torso to come up to cup her breasts.

She could see the way her whole body seemed to relax the minute his hands were on her. All she could see of him was his hands and the dark silk of his hair as he bent over to caress her neck with his lips. When he set his teeth on the nape of her neck, a shiver went through her. He grazed his way to the top of her shoulders. All the while his strong hands cupped her breasts, thumbs circling her nipples. He would brush over them and then roll them between his thumb and forefingers, and when she thought he would pinch them, when she was ready for the little flick of pain he would likely give her, he would go gentle again.

He was a sadist.

"You're tense, baby." He whispered the words in her ear, his tongue flicking her earlobe. "This is supposed to be relaxing. Am I not doing it right?"

"You know it feels amazing." Some Doms liked to tease like this. It looked like JT liked to play games. The good news was so did she. "But I need more, Sir."

Those fingers tightened lightly around her nipples. "More? More what? And I like the way you say Sir in that oh-so-posh British accent of yours."

She'd worked hard for that accent. She'd perfected it since she was originally from the country and sounded like it. It wasn't fair, but she'd known sounding cultured meant something in her world. It would mean something in JT's, too. He had an accent, but there was no questioning the man's intelligence. "You can get a bit rougher if you like, Sir."

"Rougher?" His arms tightened, pulling her back against the hard muscle of his chest. "If I like? I want you to like. How about this?"

His fingers closed around her nipples and he gave her a quick twist, sending a flare through her that went straight to her pussy. She gasped and the world seemed a bit softer than before as arousal took over and she started to forget all the reasons this was a bad idea.

"Nina, I need your words." He nipped at her earlobe. "Do you like that? Do you like me twisting your pretty little nipples? They're pink right now, but I think they'll be gorgeous when I've licked and sucked and bit them. They'll be ruby red."

"I like it very much, Sir."

He twisted her nipples again. "Watch it in the mirror. Watch how you respond to me."

She forced herself to obey, though she wanted more than anything to close her eyes and let the moment take over. But obedience was part of the agreement—even if they didn't actually have a formal agreement. She did as he asked, and the sight of those gorgeously callused hands on her skin made her tighten in anticipation. The fact that he was completely dressed and she was barely clothed did something for her. It made her feel sexy, like he couldn't wait to get his hands on her, so he'd stripped her down and hadn't bothered with his own clothes. It let her know that penetration wasn't the only thing on his mind.

It let her know he wanted to play and there were rules to the game—but there was also so much to win, and if she played right, there were no losers.

"You like a nip of pain?" He was staring at her in the mirror, his head up and eyes locked on hers.

She nodded. "I do. I like the sensation. I like the crispness of it, and then the heat that takes over. If you're serious about having sessions at night while we're at the retreat, I like a flogger with a little sting to it."

He grinned, a sexy expression. "I can handle that for you. Now tell me you won't give me hell about wearing my ring."

He was a manipulative bastard. "I'll wear whatever you want me to wear and you'll do what I tell you to do if the bullets start flying. That's the deal, Malone."

His right hand started to make its way down her body, the pads of his fingers skimming over her skin and making her tighten with anticipation. "I will honor that agreement. Now you hold still."

She watched him through the mirror as his hand slipped under the waistband of her knickers and disappeared.

"Have I told you how pretty your pussy is?"

The words were as much of a caress as the pad of his finger sliding over her. She had to catch her breath and force herself to be still for him. She could feel the hard line of his erection against her ass, the buttery soft denim of his jeans sliding against her legs because he wasn't under the same rules as she was. He wasn't still. He moved his hand, starting to explore the planes and valleys of her sex. His free arm held her tight so his hips could start a slow rhythm.

He groaned, a rumble against her ear. "You're already wet for me. You want to know how I knew you were a sweet sub? This. When I told you what I wanted from you, when I took control and you realized I was going to be good for you, this honey started to flow for me."

He was right about that. She usually took far longer to warm up. The previous night she'd written it off as it had been a long time and she'd needed the sex.

She was lying to herself. It was all about this one man. They had that elusive thing she'd started to think only existed in books and movies. They had real chemistry, the kind that revved her up and made her body hum when he walked into a room. She was drawn to him, and it was about more than his incredible body and gorgeous face. There was a warmth to the man that called to her, a sweetness and willingness to put himself out there that made her want to protect him.

He was brave with his heart, and she wanted that in her life.

But right now all she wanted was more of what he was giving her.

"That's it. You relax and let me take care of you. We don't have to worry about anything in this place but pleasure and connection." He nipped her earlobe, causing her to gasp and squirm. His free hand came up to twist her nipple, sending a thrill of erotic pain through her. "Be still. Take what I give you."

He was giving her so much. He was going to give her an orgasm, and she wasn't sure she could hold back.

Did it matter? In her world it probably did, but she was in his world and he didn't care who heard her.

Why should it matter?

She let go of everything but how he could make her feel.

Sexy. Powerful.

Beloved.

She shook off that last word because it wasn't somewhere she was willing to go yet. Maybe never. But the rest of it was beyond tempting. This was what had been missing in her other D/s relationships. She hadn't been able to totally let go with another Dom. It had always been there in the back of her mind that she needed to protect herself.

She let herself go with JT. Something deep inside told her she was safe with this man. At least her body was.

Her body was all that mattered for the moment. She was caught between his talented fingers on her pussy and that hard dick pressed against her ass. She glanced up at the mirror and JT was watching her. His eyes caught hers and she realized how much he wanted this. He wanted her to come for him. He didn't need to say the words. It was all there in his dark gaze. In the way he licked his lips like he would devour her the minute she was finished and it could be his turn.

But he wouldn't take that turn until he was sure she was satisfied. He would control himself.

Could she shake that control at some point? Could she make him as wild as he was making her?

Every muscle in her body tightened and then the glorious release hit her hard—a long wave that swept her up and away.

"Oh, the things I am about to do to you," he whispered, and she could see the predatory gleam in his eyes.

The picture they made in the mirror was stamped on her brain. He was the conqueror and she the well-satisfied prey. Yes, she would let him do anything he wanted to do to her, and she would do it with not an ounce of shame.

"Yes, Sir."

There was a knock on the door. "Uhm, Mr. Malone. I'm so sorry. There's a woman out here and I can't make her go away. I'm so sorry to bother you."

He went stiff behind her. "Nina, it might be about my father. I have to…"

She straightened up. His father's illness was the whole reason they were in the predicament they were in. Of course he was worried. "I'll get dressed and meet you out there."

"I don't think it's your mother," the saleslady said. "She said she's your assistant."

Or she could make things very easy and kill off one of the suspects.

JT ran a hand through his hair, his frustration evident. "She tracks my phone. In some places we go it's a necessary thing. I'll talk to her." He took a deep breath and groaned. "Shit. I was supposed to stop by the office and sign some contracts. I ignored her calls earlier. I'm sorry, Nina."

Somehow she thought Deanna showing up was about more than contracts.

JT leaned in and brushed his lips over hers, his mouth kicking in a wry grin before he stepped back. "But I'm pretty sure everyone knows what we're doing, and that's a good thing."

Because of their cover. That was all. He closed the door and she was left alone and almost completely naked.

If only her heart didn't feel just as bare.

* * * *

JT strode out of the dressing room, ready to throttle someone. Not someone. Deanna. He was going to fire her. Everyone wanted him to fire her, well, today was the day they all got their wish. He could handle her sharp tongue, but cock blocking was definitely where he drew the line.

She stood out in the middle of the department, a stack of files in her arms. Deanna was in her early thirties, and he was sure there were men out there who thought she was smoking hot. She had honey blonde hair and she took care of herself, but somehow he'd never been able to look at her as more than a super-competent assistant who could keep the dragons of the industry on their toes.

Attraction had hit like lightning the minute he'd seen Nina. It had been utterly unlike anything he'd felt in his life, and he was well aware that he was in too deep, way too fast, but he couldn't help himself.

"You want to explain why you're interrupting me?" It was time to reclaim some of his private life. He hadn't had much of one for years. Not since his father had backed off traveling, forcing JT to spend much of his life visiting rigs and going to conferences. He didn't do much beyond work and sleep and take the occasional morning off to play golf, which was honestly usually more about work than play. "You're going to stop tracking my phone and you're going to stop it now."

A huff came from her along with a slow frown. "How am I supposed to keep up with you? Your mother already hates me. If I lost you in a foreign country, she would really be pissed. I know everyone in the world thinks your mother is some darling, wouldn't't-hurt-a-fly-because-she's-so-classy lady, but she can be very intimidating when she wants to be. I know a cast-iron bitch when I see one."

He would have protested her calling his momma a bitch, but it was a term of respect coming from Deanna. "How about I'll stop my mother from tracking my phone? You can both follow me on social media."

"You don't ever post anything," she complained.

"Well, then you'll both have some troubled nights, won't you? Maybe she could hire a private detective to follow me around."

Deanna's expression went mulish. "Well if she did, she probably would do it because she's worried about you getting your heart ripped out of your chest by some British skank out for your money. And I know your mother is British, but she had all that Weston money behind her, so we know she married your father because she lost her damn mind, not because she needed money."

"Nina isn't a gold digger." He kept his voice down because they were out in public, and despite the fact that he was sure Deanna had sent the PI, he wasn't giving anyone more ammunition if he could help it. "She's my fiancée, and if you can't treat her with respect then we're going to have a problem."

"We'll have a problem anyway," Deanna said under her breath.

"What?"

She shook her head. "It doesn't matter. You didn't answer my texts. The stock you wanted to buy bottomed out an hour ago, but I can't give them the go-ahead to buy without your signature, and the Nikkei opens in a few hours. If we don't get it at open, we'll pay a much higher price because the sharks will be circling."

He took a deep breath. She had a good reason for hunting him down. He held out a hand. "Give it to me."

She gave him the authorization papers. "Good, because I'm worried Jordy is going to try to undercut us."

He started to look them over. "Jordy Burton? The asshole on my leadership team who was so worried about my daddy that he showed up in my hotel room this morning? That Jordy?" He knew it shouldn't surprise him.

"Yep. I'm not entirely certain, but I heard him talking to someone about stock, and he mentioned the company you've been looking at. I don't know how he knows. I wouldn't tell that massive ass a thing."

"Then why did you let him in my hotel suite?" He didn't like the idea that Jordy had somehow figured out his plans to buy up stock on a failing Japanese tech firm. They had some software that JT believed they were underusing. He wasn't certain so he wanted a deal, but if he was right, Malone Oil would have another technological edge.

So where had Jordy gotten the idea to go after the same firm?

She sighed. "I let them in because I was worried too. The Malone family closed ranks and I was on the outside. I know we're not exactly friends, JT, but I've worked for you for a long time. I spend more time with you than anyone else in the world. Forgive me for being worried."

"About me, or the company if my father dies?"

"I wouldn't worry about the company. You've been running it for the last few years. If anything, I wish you would take it all over because your dad is stubborn as the day is long and won't listen to any idea that doesn't come from a dinosaur." She gave him a pen. "Although now I'm worried because instead of dealing with this very important stock purchase you were doing something in the dressing room that made all the salesladies stand outside like they were listening to a sex show. Probably because they were."

"I get to have a private life." He finished looking through the documents and signed his name on the line.

"Not in the dressing room, you don't." She took the papers back and stepped away. "I hope you're telling me the truth and you really know this woman because I would hate to see her ruin the good work you've been doing. I'll get this filed and see you in the morning unless you're planning on ducking work to play with your…fiancée."

"I'll be there in the morning." Though he and Nina did have work to do. "Mid-morning."

Deanna sighed. "Yes, that's what I was worried about."

She turned and walked away.

"Mr. Malone, should we try more dresses?" the saleswoman asked.

He still had a ring to buy. "No. We'll take them all."

He had very little time to win Nina over. He wasn't going to waste it.

# Chapter Six

Five days later, JT stopped before the big circular drive where there would almost certainly be a valet waiting to take his truck. "Are you sure you're okay?"

"Am I okay that the last of the prep time for the op we begin tomorrow is being taken up by a sham, hastily thrown together party for a fake engagement? Of course I am."

She was not. Even he knew that. "I'm sorry. My mom thought this would be the best way to help with our cover."

His mom wanted to get a look at Nina. His mom had likely talked to Michael, who would have told her he was in way over his head, and she knew the only way to take control of the situation was to force him to come home.

They'd spent days going over and over their cover so they would have the same story of where they'd met, what their first date had been, how he'd proposed.

At a conference in London. Dinner in the West End. He'd flown into London after a month in the Middle East and asked her right there in her office.

He'd wanted something more elaborate, but she'd insisted simpler was better.

He'd taken a crash course in Nina and he was way better at studying her than he'd ever been in school. He knew she loved the color blue in all its shades. She found it soothing. She listened to a wide variety of music. She loved it when he nipped the back of her neck. It got her hot and ready in seconds.

He hated the fact that their days together were almost over. Despite the fact that he'd gone into the office, she'd joined him every day for lunch, and they'd made a couple of memories on his desk. He wouldn't ever be able to sit there again without seeing her there, her head thrown back in pure ecstasy.

But today, something had shifted and he'd begun to see more of the operative than the woman. He felt a distance opening between them, and he didn't like it one bit. "I know you wanted to talk to Big Tag. I made sure he was on the invite list. We're also bringing out some of the leadership team."

"I'm sure that will be helpful for your stock," she replied, staring at the big house ahead of them. "It's a mansion. You said it was a ranch house."

"It's on a ranch. It's a house. To me that's a ranch house."

"How many rooms?"

"Ten bedrooms. Sixteen bathrooms. You'll get a whole tour," he promised.

"Your mom understands what I'm here to do, right?"

His mother probably understood far too much, but he was taking things slow with Nina. Not physically, of course. The better phrase was likely he was laying low when it came to his future plans. As far as Nina understood, they were having fun, getting comfortable with each other for the sake of the op. She didn't know he never wanted her to take off that ring. "She thinks we're a real fake engagement. She doesn't know we're a sort of dating fake engagement."

That earned him a chuckle. "It's a bit confusing."

"Well, my mother's a lovely lady." He'd managed to avoid the introductions due to his father's health issues. His dad was stubborn as the day was long, and he'd decided he knew better than the doctors. He'd attempted to help some of the ranch hands and torn one of his incisions slightly open. His mother wasn't allowing him to leave the house until he was completely healed. "My father can be intimidating to a lot of people."

"I can handle your father. I worry this is going to be too much for him. Isn't he supposed to be resting?"

"I assure you he won't do anything he's not supposed to now," JT said. "He tends to learn from his mistakes. It's my brother I'm more worried about. Mike doesn't think I can hack this. He's probably going to take you to the side and try to convince you to trade us out."

"I won't do that. I promise you. I'm not going in without you no matter what Michael says. I trust you." She glanced at the porch. "Who is the woman?"

He watched as a diminutive figure stepped onto the porch.

"My mother." He loved her, but she was going to meddle. He could feel it from here. "She tracks my phone, too."

Nina's hand slid over his. "It's good to have people who care about you."

"Yeah, well it can be hell on a man's ego when his momma calls because she's tracked him down to a bar on the other side of the world and she wants to make sure he's safe."

Nina sighed. "I'm not close to my family at all, though I do care about them. I suppose we lost touch somewhere along the way. Go on, then. We should meet her. She's right about the party. It's going to be helpful. It gives me a reason to see Big Tag. I couldn't exactly go up to the office since we were worried about being followed. I'll get to spend time with our suspects before we're with the whole leadership team. I'm sure Big Tag can tell us if it was your assistant who hired the PI."

He took his foot off the brake and started for the house. "I know it was her. I'll have to fire her when this is over. I hate that."

"If she's not the spy, you don't have to fire her."

But he did if she was setting private investigators on his girlfriends. He had to wonder if she'd done it before. He'd never had a girlfriend who would pick up on a tail. "We'll see."

"JT, you don't have to do anything at all. You understand that, right? You don't even have to do this mission if you would rather not. I don't want the Agency to push you into something you feel uncomfortable with."

Did she not think he could do it? "I'll be fine. I want to catch this person more than anyone. This is my company and I worked on that prototype, but there's more. I've got skin in this game because Bill was my friend no matter what dipshit thing he did."

"I know, and that's why I'm a bit worried about you. You're a good man. Sometimes this is a rough business on a good man."

"You're not exactly bad."

"No, but I think I likely have a more flexible sense of morality."

"What is that supposed to mean? I don't understand what's happening here. We've had a great week together, but I've felt you pulling away all day," he admitted. "If it's not about the job, then it has to be about me."

For a moment he thought he'd pushed her too far. She stared straight ahead and he worried she would simply open the door and leave him sitting there. But then she turned her head slightly. "It's not about you. There are things I haven't told you, things you should know. I've been used before. You should understand that the reason I work for McKay-Taggart and Knight is because I was fired from my last job. I was involved with a man I worked with."

There was a knock on his window. The valet was smiling at him.

JT stared and the man backed off.

"You don't have to tell me anything you don't want to."

"No. You should understand before going in with me. It's a simple story." Her voice had gone wooden. This was a story she'd likely had to tell far too many times. "I fell in love with my partner. We worked for Interpol. We had been partners for several years. I thought we would get married and have a family. He thought I was excellent cover for his real job, which was taking care of his drug lord employer so his crimes never came to light. Despite the fact that I turned him in, they were right to sack me. I was lucky Damon was willing to take a chance on me. So that's why I don't sleep with clients or coworkers. But we weren't coworkers at the time. At least we didn't know it."

He was glad it had already gotten dark or she might have seen him flush with shame. He'd known. "Nina, this is not the same. And you're not using me. I know you think I'm naïve, but I know damn well when a woman wants something out of me. I'm sorry I pushed. I like you a lot."

She smiled weakly. "I like you, too."

"And that's part of the problem."

"It is."

So she'd gotten burned and didn't trust herself. He had no plans to use her at all. Yes, he should have backed off when he'd figured out she was his contact, but she didn't have to know he knew. Some things were better left unsaid. He could be good for her if she let him. But she needed to make that decision for herself. "Are you asking me to back off? Are you saying you've decided you don't want us to go any further?"

He wasn't sure what he would do if she said yes.

She sighed. "I don't know. I wanted you to understand. I'm not telling you no."

"You're not telling me yes, either." He didn't say it with any kind of accusation. It was merely the truth.

"I'm saying I would like to think about it. What we have is very new. It's fragile."

"And I don't want to break it." He put the truck in park.

Her hand went over his. "Can't we just live in the moment?"

He wasn't good at that. "Sure."

Her hand tightened around his. "I don't have to pretend like I want to spend every minute of the night looking at you. I'm afraid it's going to be far too easy to look like a woman who's crazy about a man."

She knew how to ease him. He brought her hand to his lips. "I'll give you all the time you need."

He let her go and got out of the truck to face the music.

* * * *

Nina decided that JT's mother must be the queen of entertaining since as far as she knew this small party to celebrate a very fake engagement had been thrown together hastily. She'd had mere days, and yet everything was lovely, from the gorgeous flowers in the foyer to the champagne fountain that was set up in what someone had called the grand salon.

The rich were truly different.

But then her son worked fast, too. He'd only had five days, but he'd managed to work his way into her life. Five days of being close to him had made her like him so much. Five nights in his bed and she'd come to crave him. They hadn't exactly played yet, though there was no question he was dominant in the bedroom.

What would he be like in a club? What would it feel like to scene with him?

She had such dangerous thoughts.

"Nina, dear, it's so good to have you here." Ava Malone was a gorgeous woman who looked far younger than her sixty-five years. She wore a chic cocktail dress that showed off toned arms and a trim waist. "Finally. When Deanna told me your truck was pulling up the drive, I was so excited."

She pointedly said JT's assistant's name, and sure enough, the woman was already here, a frown on her face and a drink in her hand. She was staring their way.

JT slid in behind Nina, his hand on the small of her back in that possessive way that made her melt for the right man.

She'd thought Roger was the right man. It was good to remind herself of that.

"I'm thrilled to be here. How is Mr. Malone doing? Is there any way I can help you?" The poor woman hadn't asked to be brought into this situation.

She caught a glimpse of Michael Malone and realized that she probably had been asked. Michael had a look on his face that made her suspicious this party might not have been Ava's plan at all.

Ava Malone waved her off. "Not at all. I could use a distraction from that ornery old man. My husband is a bear when he's sick, though you should know he's feeling much better this evening. Although I haven't told him about the new diet yet. And you look stunning. Don't worry about a thing. JT, could you please come with me to make sure he hasn't bullied the waitstaff into giving him Scotch? Nina, love, I'm going to borrow JT for a moment if that's all right."

Ah, so she wanted to talk to JT alone. Or perhaps not totally alone since she could see Michael beginning to make his way over.

JT looked her way, uncertainty plain on his face. "I don't know that I should throw Nina to the wolves."

Oh, but wolves were her specialty. She thought she might have more of a chance to get a real impression of some of her suspects without JT there with her. "I'll be fine."

"I'll have him back before dinner," Ava promised.

JT stared back at her before letting his mom lead him away.

It was obvious JT had trouble telling the women in his life what to do. That was likely because he'd been raised by an alpha female and taught to respect feminine authority.

Except in the bedroom. There he had no trouble mastering a woman.

JT was a nice guy. She had no doubt that he could run his business, but they were dealing with her business now, and perhaps it was time to be a good partner to him.

She stepped in front of Michael Malone before he could follow his brother and mother. "A word please, Mr. Malone."

Michael was wearing slacks and a button-down shirt, his dark hair slicked back. "I need to talk to my brother, Nina."

"Oh, I think you need to leave your brother alone. If you push him, you'll upset him, and I need him calm and ready to work. I understand that he's your family but for now he's my partner."

Michael stepped back, his shoulders relaxing as though he understood he wasn't going anywhere until she was satisfied. "He's not up to this assignment. You should let me go in with you. I can get you my dossier if you need it."

"You're Michael Malone. You grew up wealthy, went to the best schools. You attended the University of Texas Austin and received a degree in management while your brother studied petroleum engineering. Shortly after your graduation, you signed up for the Navy, much to the shock and surprise of your family. You rose quickly through the ranks and became a SEAL within three years of your commission. You served honorably around the world before you were recruited by CIA operative Tennessee Smith to his private elite team. Though you were never formally CIA, you worked exclusively for them for a solid year before Mr. Smith was fired. You chose to leave the Navy and begin employment with McKay-Taggart where you've worked the last several years. Did they offer you a position in the Agency?"

A single brow had arched over Michael's eyes. "They did. They offered me Ten's job, but I would have been working under a man known as Levi Green. I didn't like him. I also had seen how they treated their operatives. I knew it would be hard to go back to straight military work."

"You had a taste for the spy life."

"I had a taste for using my brain and not having to merely follow orders."

She suspected there was far more to it, but she wouldn't press him. "Tell me something. Was it expected that you would come home and run the business side of Malone Oil while JT worked the research and exploration side?"

A slight flush to his cheeks told her what she needed to know before he said the words. "Yes. That was the plan. I couldn't go through with it."

"So you left JT to handle the whole thing?"

"JT loved the company. I did not. It wasn't my thing. I get to have a life of my own."

"Then have it, Mr. Malone, and stop trying to force your brother into the same mold your parents tried to force you into. He's perfectly capable of following my orders. He's competent to do this job. Stop trying to treat him like he needs protection."

"He does," Michael insisted.

"That's what I'm here for. If you need me to, I'll send you my dossier."

He frowned. "This is the part where I really wish I could bounce that right back at you, but the truth is I didn't study you. I trusted Ian and Damon."

She'd rather thought that was the case. "Tell me why you weren't worried about your father, but you're terrified for your brother."

"Because my father would let you do your job. My father would understand that you're here to protect him. My brother is a great guy, but he's got a real thing about protecting women."

"He assures me he'll be fine hiding behind me if the bullets start to fly."

Michael shook his head. "He won't. He'll jump right in front of you. He'll tell you what you want to hear. Hell, he might even believe it, but I know him. You're sleeping with him, right?"

"I didn't know who he was when I went up to his room that first night," she began.

Michael held up his hands as if conceding. "Hey, no judgment here. You're both adults. But you have to know he…" He stopped himself. "JT isn't the kind of man who has a lot of one-night stands. I often joke that he's got a biological clock and it's ticking hard. He can get in deep really fast. Another reason to take me instead."

Except it could truly hurt JT if she asked him to do it. And there were other problems with that scenario. "You don't know the business the way he does. You might be able to pretend to be him in a casual way, but what happens when they get down to numbers?"

"I can work my way through it," Michael insisted.

"I will take care of him."

"He might not let you." Michael took a deep breath and seemed to come to a decision. "Look, we had this friend growing up. Her name was Dana."

Yes, she'd heard the name before. JT hadn't mentioned her again. They'd talked about a lot of things over the days they'd spent together, but until earlier this evening neither had mentioned prior relationships. She'd been so curious about Dana since the name had been said with deep sorrow. "He loved her?"

"Not exactly, though I think he always figured they would get married one day. She was our father's best friend's daughter. We grew up with her. Our parents always talked about Dana marrying one of us and joining our families. JT thought it would be him. I don't think he ever loved her. Not in an in-love way, but they were close when they were kids."

She got a sinking feeling in the pit of her stomach. There could only be one reason for that aching sorrow she'd heard in JT's voice. "She's not around anymore, is she?"

"She was a lot like me. I know I seem hard on my brother, but I know what I did hurt him. Dana rebelled, too. She went a little wild and ended up marrying someone she shouldn't have. She went missing when we were in college. We've never found her, and we've had the best in the business look. It was like she disappeared off the face of the earth. It affected JT. It affected me, too, but I accepted long ago that I can't control the world around me. JT hasn't learned that lesson. He didn't have to because he does control his world."

"That's not fair. He's had to because he didn't have anyone to lean on. Don't get me wrong. I'm not blaming you for the choices you've made, but you left him. I suspect up until that moment you did almost everything together. Did you ever talk to him about the fact that all that responsibility, all that destiny, suffocated you?"

"He wouldn't have understood," Michael insisted. "He wanted it. He wanted everything our parents had planned for us. He would have tried to stop me, and I couldn't let that happen. I had to break free. I had to find out who I was without the Malone name behind me."

"Then you should understand how he feels. He needs to know he can do this. If you force him out, I think you'll hurt your relationship with him."

"But your job would be far easier with me." His eyes narrowed. "Unless there's a reason you specifically want JT on this. Are you looking to spend more time with him?"

"I think he's the best man for the job." She wasn't about to let Michael put her in a corner. "I think I can handle him. Now that I know what will worry him, I'll manage him better. I appreciate that information. If you're questioning whether or not I'll let some attraction to your brother mess with this op…"

He shook his head. "No. I know you wouldn't do that. Again, I trust our bosses. But you like him. You like JT."

She was about to protest that liking JT Malone didn't matter when a feminine voice broke her concentration.

"I would hope she likes JT if she's planning on marrying him." Deanna stood right behind Michael, eyeing them both like she wasn't sure what she'd walked up on.

Well, it proved that she wasn't entirely on her game since normally she would never break cover unless she was completely alone. "Michael was making fun of his brother. He seems to do that a lot."

Michael shrugged and smiled smoothly. "It's been my hobby since we were kids. I can't help it. I'm the pretty one and the smart one."

Nice deflection. He knew what he was doing. "I hardly think you're prettier than him."

"He's definitely not smarter since he walked away from a billion-dollar empire for the military." Deanna had a glass of red wine in her hand. "And honestly, I can't tell the difference between the two of them until they open their mouths, and then Michael sounds like he's a paranoid nut bag."

Michael frowned her way. "Really?"

"Duh, you're always going on about spies and stuff. No one is trying to steal our oil rigs. They're kind of too big to steal," Deanna said. "But you get JT all riled up and then I have to calm him down."

Michael sighed, obviously unwilling to start this fight. "I think I'll go check on my dad. Thank you, Nina. You've given me a lot to think about. I think you're going to be very good for my brother."

She wasn't sure what he meant by that, or if he was merely playing his part. She only hoped she'd gotten through to the man. "Hello, Deanna. I would have thought you would take the day off since you've been around so very often."

"Expect to see me a lot," Deanna replied, a smug smirk on her face. "I'm not some nine to fiver. I'm on a path and I'm not about to let anyone push me off that path, if you know what I mean, Ms. Banks from London. You've never been married. That's surprising, given your age."

She laughed. The queen bee shite didn't get to her at all. "I'm in my thirties and I've had a career. You're what? Thirty-three at the very least."

"Yes, but I've been married before," she replied.

"And now you're divorced."

Deanna tipped her glass. "Happily. You're older than JT."

"Slightly. Or are you one of those people who view women in dog years? Like we're only interesting when we're twenty, and every year after that is accelerated rot? Like I said, you're not that far behind me, darling."

"No, I'm not far behind you at all, Nina Banks. You should remember that. If you try to force me out, think about the fact that he can't get through a day without me. You might amuse him in dressing rooms, but you can't do what I do. I know you've worked for some communications company in Europe, but this is America and this is the oil business. You stay in your lane and I'll stay in mine." She turned and strode away.

Nina really hoped it was Deanna. It would be fun to shoot her at the end of all of this.

"Don't pay any attention to her." One of the men she'd met that first morning in JT's suite approached her, two glasses of wine in his hands. He was dressed in a suit, his hair mussed in that way that was supposed to look casual but actually took quite a bit of work. He offered her one of the glasses. "She's been angling for JT's attention since he hired her. If you ask me, she got divorced so she would be available for him. Poor thing."

Jordy Burton. She took the glass, though she wouldn't drink a sip of it. "I'm not worried about her, Mr....?"

Nina Blunt, badass operative, knew everything about this man. Badass operative knew that he'd served on the board of Malone Oil for five years, ever since his father had retired and transferred all that stock to his only son. She knew that Jordy Burton spent the majority of his time mountain climbing or surfing or white-water rafting. He was an adrenaline junkie.

But Nina Banks, sweet fiancée to JT Malone, likely wouldn't even remember his full name.

Jordy had the arrogance to look annoyed. "Jordan Burton. We met earlier this week."

She gave him what she hoped was a flustered smile. "Sorry. This week has been a whirlwind. That first morning was difficult. Jet lag and all."

"Must not travel a lot," Jordy said with a superior smile. "My body is perfectly used to going from time zone to time zone, but that's because I've trained it well. Proper nutrition and excellent DNA. I recently returned from Nepal. I was going to try Everest, but it's gotten so touristy, you know."

She nodded, her brain churning because maybe his dossier didn't tell the whole truth. Any real climber would know Everest's summit was only accessible in April and May, depending on the weather. If he recently returned from Nepal, he hadn't been attempting to summit Everest.

"I prefer K2," Jordy continued. "It's actually tougher. Says more about the climber, you know."

"Have you traveled extensively through Asia? It's a part of the world I've always wanted to see." As long as she was here, she might as well start asking some subtle questions. If she could find a way to narrow down their suspects, they could focus in. Keeping eyes on one or two suspects would be far easier than three. She was already starting to discount Deanna. It wasn't that she didn't believe the woman capable of murder. She seemed cold enough, but she also had shown loyalty to her employer. Maybe it was about wanting JT on a personal level, but women didn't tend to stab the men they wanted in the back. At least not until they'd been rejected. If Deanna still had hopes of her goal, she doubted the woman would risk blowing it all up.

But the man in front of her was a different animal altogether.

"I've been everywhere," Jordy bragged. "I could show you all the best places in Asia. They've got casinos there that make Vegas look like a church preschool."

"I bet," she replied with a smile. "Like I said, I've always wanted to visit. I have a friend who lives in Busan. She transferred there a few months ago, but I haven't had the chance to see her new place."

"Ah, yes, Korea. I've been several times. I've got friends in all the right places, if you know what I mean."

"I don't."

He lowered his voice and leaned in. "I know people in the consulate, if you want to go. They can get you into any place you want. You and JT should think about it for your honeymoon."

Well, she would certainly think about it. If he had contacts with the South Korean embassy, she wanted to connect those dots and see who else they connected to. "Why don't you tell me about your friends? I've got a couple of friends at the British consulate."

"Oh, I'm in good with all the politicos. If there was one thing my dad taught me, it was to be cool with both sides of the spectrum," Jordy replied. "I donate to everyone so they're all in my pocket. It's why I keep up all these board positions. I don't need to work at all, but it's important to keep friends in high places."

She would be surprised if this man could keep a secret long enough to be an effective spy. "Yes, I can see where that would be helpful."

She glanced up and saw a familiar face walking her way. Charlotte Taggart did not look like a woman who had recently had a baby. She wore a killer sheath that clung to her every curve, her strawberry blonde hair in curls around her shoulders.

"Ms. Banks," she said with a smile on her face. "It's good to see you again."

Jordy took a step back, as though he wouldn't get too close to the gorgeous redhead. "Mrs. Taggart, I wasn't aware you knew JT's fiancée. That's surprising since none of the rest of us did."

"It's not surprising at all," Charlotte replied smoothly. "Who do you think vetted her when she started dating JT? Do you honestly believe JT wouldn't run a check on someone he's getting serious about? My husband was in England a few months ago. He was there to ensure that Ms. Banks is exactly who she says she is. A man in JT's position can never be too careful. Haven't you learned that?"

Jordy huffed and turned away, walking toward a small group of men in suits with tumblers of Scotch in their hands.

Charlotte leaned in. "He got taken by a con artist a couple of years back. Wiped out his trust fund. Lucky for him his dad had more money than god and bailed him out. In the last few years his father has had a couple of cancer treatments, and Jordy has taken over the board seats. I fear what happens when the dad dies and he gets control of that cash."

She started walking the way Charlotte led, glancing back to ensure no one was listening. "He claims to have connections in South Korea."

"Maybe, but you should know he lies a lot. They all do." Charlotte led her across the grand hallway and back toward a smaller room. "The board members are a lot like a nest of snakes, but most of them have held their seats forever, so the Malones know how to handle them. Tell me something. Has Deanna shown her claws yet?"

"She's taken a swipe," Nina replied. "I'm fairly certain she set the PI on us, though apparently she tracks JT's phone."

"They are a little on the codependent side. JT lets her run a lot of his day-to-day life, but he is super private when it comes to anything outside of business." Charlotte opened the door. "It's why this can actually work. JT dated a woman from Sanctum up until a few months ago and Deanna never even knew her name."

He'd had a sub? She wasn't sure why the thought surprised her. She knew he was a Dom and he had been for a while. Why wouldn't he have had a sub or two?

She'd never had a Dom. She'd played and had sessions with some of the Doms at The Garden, but she'd never worn a collar.

"That's good to know."

Charlotte opened the door and there was already a conversation going on.

"You need to talk to your monster, Ian," Alex McKay was saying. "She doesn't have to be mean to Cooper."

Tag rolled his baby blues. "Seriously? What did she do now?"

"She told their whole class that Coop has cooties," Alex complained.

"He doesn't anymore. We got rid of the lice, that might I point out, Kala gave him. She was ground zero in that particular outbreak."

Charlotte leaned over. "Kala might have found a cap in the trash outside of the club. She decided to wear it. Then she took it to Alex and Eve's and put it on Cooper. It was not a fun time." She walked fully into the room and addressed Alex. "I'll talk to her about that. You know I think it's because she's got a little crush on Cooper."

Ian put a hand on his stomach as though something was going to come back up. "No, she doesn't. The only thing my baby girl is crushing on is life itself. She's killing it at karate. All she was doing was warning the world that Coop had the nits."

"Carys told me Coop had been talking to another little girl when Kala made her announcement." Eve McKay rounded out the foursome, all of them dressed for the cocktail party. It was a bit intimidating to be around Eve McKay. Charlotte Taggart tended to view the world as one big soap opera being played out for her pleasure, but Eve took everything seriously and through a psychologist's eye.

She hadn't been at McKay-Taggart and Knight for very long. Was Eve here to ensure she wouldn't screw things up?

Charlotte nodded as though she'd thought that was what had happened. "Alice Diaz. She's adorable, and I couldn't figure out why Kala hates her until now. And she's definitely crushing on Cooper no matter what Ian says."

Ian had his fingers in his ears. "Lies. Lies, I tell you."

Alex stood near Ian. "No one wants that to be true less than I do." He glanced Nina's way. "Sorry. The kiddos are starting to show signs of pairing off, and it's freaking the rest of us out."

"I thought it was funny when it happened to Sean," Ian said with a frown. "He's going to end up with Jake and Adam and Liam for in-laws if he doesn't shut that shit down. As for my baby girl, Kala will be too busy saving the world ninja style to date. I'm afraid I've given up on Kenz. She's too much like her momma. All I've asked is that she bring home an American." He shuddered. "I couldn't handle it if she brought home some stuffy Brit or worse."

"What's worse than a stuffy Brit?" Alex asked.

"Canadian," Ian retorted. "With their politeness and weird bacon. I fear the Canadian more than any other."

Charlotte was the one rolling her eyes now. "Can we cut the kid talk and focus on the actual Brit in our midst?"

Big Tag grinned. "Nina's not stuffy. I heard she took her last bullet like a champ. Avoided the roofie the bad guy slipped into her tea but took one to the chest."

"Well if I'd known he was going to shoot me, I would have had the tea," she admitted and held up the wine she'd taken from one of their suspects. "Speaking of drinks, I'm not about to drink this. It's probably fine, but once roofied, twice shy and all that."

Charlotte took the glass from her. "I can find something for you. This house has a bar in almost every room. I've always liked the Malones. How is it going between you and JT?"

"We get along quite well," she replied.

"How was the shopping?" Charlotte asked, expectation in her tone.

"It was fine. We've been three times this week. Apparently, I need a lot of clothes." It had been paradise. Everywhere they'd gone the world had opened up and invited her in. Or rather JT. Back in London, she could barely get the bloke who ran the register at Tesco to look up from his phone. "We got everything we need for the retreat. Well, everything we need that we can get at a shopping mall. I assume Sandra and Hutch have all of our equipment, including my gun. I don't want to take it with me in case security decides I look sketchy."

Charlotte studied her for a moment and then sighed. "I hate it when Ian's right."

Ian smirked. "I told you she was into him."

"I'm not into him." She wasn't about to tell the man she'd slept with the client all week.

Charlotte shook her head. "If you weren't into him, you would have been more excited about the shopping. Unlike Alex and Eve, Ian and I have spent time with you. You flipped out when you got to escort that pop star around Harrods, and you didn't even get to buy anything."

It had been such fun to watch the young woman shop. She'd been bright and peppy and kind. She really should have enjoyed the shopping more, but every time they went to a store her mind had been on JT. "I'm not into him."

"I wouldn't be surprised if you were," Eve said from her place next to her husband. "JT is one of the nicest men I've ever met. Knowing what I know about him and what I know about you, I would say you're a decent match on paper."

"I'm still confused about how we went from Nina going in as an assistant to fiancée. I get that she couldn't go in as JT's assistant, but fiancée is a big leap," Alex said.

Ian waved that off. "I can tell you what happened. JT saw her and decided he wanted in her pants. Excuse me. Knickers. He got all flusterpated, and next thing you know they're engaged. Is everyone buying it?"

"They seem to be," Charlotte replied. "Ava is selling it, though you should know they're talking about you being a gold digger."

She shrugged. "That was inevitable. It's good because at least they're not talking about me being a former Interpol officer. Is my Nina Banks ID holding up?"

Big Tag seemed to get serious, and he crossed to the bar where he opened the bottle of Scotch. "So far it's solid, but Adam is worried because someone used that name on the Deep Web. He's got some contacts he keeps up, and someone is looking to break your cover. They don't have anything yet, but it definitely goes beyond what the PI did. From what I can tell he ran a skip trace on you and spent that first afternoon tailing you. Has he followed you since?"

"I haven't seen him again," she promised. She didn't like the idea that someone was going deeper. "It could ruin the whole op if they connect me to Interpol."

"Yeah, well I have no one else to send in," Tag said, offering her a glass. She took it. This one she would drink. "Everyone knows Charlie and Eve, and Erin was willing to go but Theo was a whiny manbaby."

"She just gave birth, Ian," Charlotte pointed out.

Big Tag's lips quirked up. "Two weeks ago. She's already bugging me to send her on assignment. You can't keep that chick caged, but she's got a problem. Unfortunately, despite his maternal nature, Theo can't actually produce breast milk, though he's got some solid B-cups after all that sympathetic eating."

The women all frowned Tag's way, but Alex had a solid laugh.

"Sorry," Alex said in a not-sorry way. "Theo was insufferable. It makes me almost glad he was dead the first time around."

Eve rounded on her husband. "Too soon, Alex. It will always be too soon to joke about that."

Alex held his hands up like he was warding off an attack. "I said almost. Come on, angel. Theo's been obnoxious. He was a walking, talking encyclopedia of pregnancy, and he lorded it over everyone. Like the rest of us haven't been around pregnant women. I had to deal with your surprise pregnancy and we had an infant. There's barely nine months between Hunter and Vivian."

Eve's lips curled up as she turned Nina's way. "I didn't think I could get pregnant so we adopted two boys, Cooper and Hunter. A couple of days after we brought Hunter home, I found out that miracles happen, and that's how we ended up with three kiddos when we were pretty sure we wouldn't have any." She shifted back to her husband. "And Erin was in the same situation. Give them a break. It's perfectly reasonable he would be a little obsessed."

Alex waved her off. "Well, he's still obsessed. You watch it. He's going to be the ultimate helicopter parent to that little girl. But seriously, Erin would have been wrong for this particular job. She would have threatened the suspects until they all confessed and we wouldn't be any closer to figuring it out. Also, she would have driven JT insane. Don't worry about the Deep Web inquiries. They won't have time to figure out who you really are. Adam worked with Hutch on the construct. It'll hold."

She hoped it would. "Everyone's in place at the resort?"

"Hutch and Sandra are already down there, and apparently Drake flies in tonight," Tag replied. "Watch him. I don't trust anyone in the Agency after what happened with Solo. Try to remember who Drake's working for."

No one she trusted. "I will."

"And don't forget about fake pregnancies," Tag continued.

She groaned and thanked fate Tag wasn't coming along.

\* \* \* \*

"She's lovely," Ava Malone said as they walked toward his father's study. "According to Michael she's very competent. He says she's former Interpol."

JT sent his mother a frustrated glare. "We don't exactly want anyone to know that."

She waved him off. "No one can hear us in this hall. Trust me. I know every inch of this house and how sound reverberates. Your teenage years taught me that."

He had the grace to wince. He and his brother had been good at sneaking out. Not so great at sneaking back in. "How is Dad?"

She stopped in front of the big portrait of his great granddad. She put a hand on his shoulder. "He's fine. He's quite healthy. I'm not worried about him except for the fight we'll have the next time he orders chicken fried steak. I'm worried about you. My darling, have you thought about this?"

His heart sank a bit, though he should have known this was coming. "I'm not going to let someone get away with stealing from us."

His mother's jaw tightened. "It's more than that and you know it. Someone killed William Murphy. Mr. Taggart is certain of it."

He wasn't going to have this conversation twice. He pushed through the door that led to where his father was sitting in his big comfy chair, his massive German shepherd at his side. The poor dog had whined and cried when his master had been in pain, and he'd been miserable to be apart from him.

Maybe he should get a dog. The dog would love him and not question his every move. The dog might have faith that he could handle himself.

Nina seemed to think he could.

"JT, you need to tell your mother I'm not some old man who can't do for himself," his father said.

"Mother, he's not some old man who had surgery a few days ago and needs someone who loves him to take care of him. Let him die." His father responded best to tough love. Lord knew the old man could dish it out.

"That is not what I said," his father insisted.

He needed to make a few things plain, and very quickly. "Dad, you let your health get away from you. Your doctor has been telling you for years this would happen. You were lucky it was your gall bladder and not your heart. We thought we were going to lose you, and not a one of us has gotten over that yet. You sit in that chair and you do everything the docs and Mom tell you to do because we love you. Because you love us, and you know we need you to be safe."

His father's expression softened. "All right."

He turned to his mother. "You take care of Dad and stop worrying about me. I'm not Michael, but I'm not some wilting flower either, and I'm sick of being treated like the delicate one in this family. You trust me to run this business?"

"You know I do," his mother replied.

"Then you let me run it, and that includes protecting it from spies. I do not want anyone to try to talk me out of a fight I need to have."

His mother's manicured hands came up in apology. "You're right. I'm sorry. I can only use the same excuse I use on your father. I love you.

I'm worried about you."

"Were you worried about me when I was on a rig in the middle of the Arabian Sea?"

"Absolutely. Every single day," she assured him.

"She was a mess the entire time you were gone," his dad agreed. "She doesn't think you're incapable, son. She's your mom. She's always worried about you."

It was worse than he'd thought. "She's not worried about Mike."

His dad snorted. "Are you kidding? You do know your mom has your brother's partner's phone number, right? She gets updates when they're on assignment. It isn't hard. When he's working with that Bear fellow, she intimidates him."

He could guess what she used on the other guy Michael routinely worked with. "She sends Boomer food."

"Mr. Boomer is a very reasonable lad." His mother fussed over his dad, straightening his blanket and making sure his feet were covered. "I send him a few treats and he gives me updates."

It was good to know he wasn't the only one his mother treated like a child.

Maybe it was time to accept that the worry came with the love.

He would worry about sending Nina to deal with the spy. Yes, she was competent and capable, but that didn't mean he wouldn't worry. "All right. Know that I promise to be careful. Dad, you've had time to think about this. Do you have any ideas who this could be? I know the list of suspects, but I have trouble believing any of them would steal this way."

"You're too trusting," his father replied. "Honestly, it could be any one of them. I would hate to find out it's Deanna, but she lied about being in Houston."

"There could be reasons for that," he countered.

"I don't understand the appeal." His mother shook her head and walked over to the small bar. She poured two glasses. "She's a harpy."

"Yes, so JT doesn't have to be." His dad frowned as his mom passed one glass to JT and kept the other for herself. "If Michael had taken his place in the company, he could have been the bad guy. Someone has to be."

"Good god, are we on this again?" Michael walked into the room, straight past JT to the booze.

"Hey, son," his dad began.

"Nope." Michael poured out a single glass. "I'm way more scared of

Mom than you, and has anyone considered the fact that I didn't go into the family business because I was tired of always being the bad guy? Also, I never considered myself the bad guy. I was the rational, logical guy. When you think about it, it all worked out because Deanna loves to be the bad guy. She's good at it. As for her being our spy, I doubt it. I know my initial instinct is that I don't like her so it's probably her, but she's been loyal to the company."

"She didn't have a reason to be in Houston," his mother pointed out.

But he could think of a few. "Have we checked to see if she interviewed with any of our competitors?" It was something he'd been pondering since the moment he'd realized her name was on that list. Houston was the headquarters of many an oil and natural gas company. "She's getting impatient. When she started with me, she told me her five-year plan was to move into management. It's been seven years and I haven't moved her where she should be for the simple fact that I need her. She does exactly what you said she does. She's a brick wall between me and the hard decisions."

"Well, I never said she wasn't smart." His father frowned at him. "You need to find a place for her. She's valuable and she knows the business every bit as well as you do."

"I can't stand that woman." His mother took a long swallow, proving she'd learned how to drink like a true Texan.

"You don't have to like her to admit she's effective." He couldn't see this being Deanna, though she had set a PI on him. "She hired a PI to follow me."

Michael huffed a laugh. "She doesn't need a PI to track you. No one does. Deanna was tracking Nina. She's trying to prove she's not who she says she is. And she isn't, so that's a problem. Tag is probably talking to Nina right now about the fact that we've got a real pro looking into her cover."

His gut tightened. "Another investigator?"

Michael shook his head. "Another spy. Likely the one we're dealing with, the man who's planning on turning over your prototype to North Korea."

The one who had probably killed Bill. He was looking into Nina.

Michael pointed his way. "This. That right there. That's why I think you should back out of this op. You think it's because I'm worried you'll fuck it up, and you're right. But you're wrong about the why. I don't think you're incapable. I think you're in too deep with Nina and that will put you both in danger."

"In too deep?" His mother had perked up considerably. "With that lovely British girl?"

"She's hardly a girl, and this is none of Mike's business." The last thing he needed was his mom to start getting visions of grandbabies in her head. He was trying not to scare Nina off.

"It is exactly my business since she's my team member," Michael insisted.

"I thought you never met her."

"That doesn't mean she's not on my team. I know this business, brother. It can be hard to have a partner in danger, much less someone you have a romantic attachment to."

"Romantic attachment?" His mother had forgotten about the Scotch. "I thought you only met her recently."

"A man knows when it's right," his father declared, reaching for her hand. "I knew the minute I met your momma that I would marry her. Where's my future daughter-in-law? I want to see her."

JT sent his brother a stare that he hoped properly expressed how much he wanted to murder him. "I wasn't planning on telling them Nina and I are seeing each other."

"Are you? Does she know?" his father asked.

"How can she not know?" His mother had taken his father's hand, as though awaiting some tragedy. "JT, you have to tell women you like them. You can't expect them to read your mind. Flowers work."

"I think she can probably read his dick," Michael said under his breath.

"Nina knows I'm interested in her." He needed to throw his parents off the scent or they would have his baby pictures out before dinner this evening. "We're taking it slow."

"You've known her for a week. We're at your engagement party, brother. You're not taking it slow. This is a bullet train," Michael replied. "And I'm worried it's going to derail if you're not careful. Mom, can I steal JT for a moment? I heard the housekeeper say dinner was almost ready."

His mother sighed. "Well, then I should go and make sure the dining room is properly set. Come along, love. I'll get you settled and we can…talk to some of our guests."

His father winced as he got to his feet. "I don't know why I have to go. You won't let me eat anything."

"I've got a lovely beef consommé for you to start with," his mother promised as she started to lead him out. The dog followed gamely behind them.

"I don't even know what that is," his father complained.

His mother sighed as she closed the door behind them.

"He's going to make her crazy," Michael muttered. "It's soup, obviously. He knows that."

"You stay out of my relationship with Nina." He had to draw firm boundaries with his brother. "I don't know why you've got it in your head that you need to stick your nose in this, but I've got it handled. I'm not going to screw up this mission."

"But you are. You already have."

He wished he'd never agreed to this party. "What is that supposed to mean?"

"It means this was supposed to be an easy cover," Michael pointed out. "She was going in as an assistant. We could have found another place for her. She still could have gone in as a staff member. Hell, she could still have gone in as Dad's assistant. Did you think of that? She could have gone down to take notes for him. No one would have questioned it at all. No one would have even noticed her, but you had to turn a spotlight her way. That's the worst thing in the world for a spy."

He didn't like the thought of Nina being in the shadows. "She's handling it fine."

"She shouldn't have had to."

"What was I supposed to do? I didn't plan on Deanna, Jordy, and Patrick showing up on my doorstep," he argued. "I was out getting us breakfast or I assure you I would have protected her."

Michael pointed like JT had just made his point. "And she wouldn't have answered the damn door in the first place if she hadn't been distracted by you."

It would have bought her a little time, but Deanna could be insistent. She wouldn't have left simply because no one answered the door. "I'm sorry you think I screwed this up, but Nina herself told them we were involved. It was the only thing that made sense at the time. I couldn't say she was a casual hookup and bring her along to the retreat."

Michael frowned. "And you couldn't let her not go to the retreat because you couldn't stand the thought of not seeing her again."

"Nina made that decision." He wasn't about to admit that he would have done anything to keep her close. "You're not going to get me to change my mind. I'm going to find out who murdered Bill and stole our tech."

"I thought you were going to let Nina handle everything."

"I'm going to help her. That's what I meant. I'm going to give her the cover she needs to figure it out."

"I wish I could believe you." Michael was quiet for a moment. "I told her about Dana."

His heart tightened when he heard her name, but he'd come to an uneasy acceptance. "I know she's not Dana. I know this isn't anything like what happened with Dana. Nina isn't a nineteen-year-old rebel who picks the wrong men. And I hope you didn't make it seem like I was crazy in love with her. She was my friend, my best friend most of my life."

Michael seemed to soften. "I know. She was mine, too. I wish she was with us, but we have to move on. *You* have to move on. I wonder if the reason you haven't gotten serious is you're still mourning Dana."

It was hard to mourn when they'd never found her body. He'd accepted that she wasn't coming home, but it was hard to never know what happened. "You're not exactly dripping in long-term women yourself."

A hint of a smile crossed his brother's face. "I'm not interested in getting married. But you are. You're the one who always wanted a family."

He didn't see why that was a problem. "I'm not jumping on the first woman I see, if that's what you're insinuating."

"I know. The truth is I like her," Michael admitted. "I like the fact that she's already willing to back you up even when it comes to me."

"She is?"

"She pretty much told me to mind my own damn business and to stop treating you like a child."

Good for Nina. "Maybe you should listen to her." He sighed. He hated that the last few years had been somewhat tense between them. "I really like this woman. I want to see where things can go. I promise I won't screw this up and I won't do anything that could put her in more danger. That's the very last thing I want."

Michael stared his way for a moment as though trying to figure out how to handle him. "I know that's your intention. You need to remember that she's the expert at this. Not you." He was quiet for a moment. "She thinks you didn't know who she was when you met her at the hotel. But Genny sent you her dossier and a picture. Genny also told you she'd be at the same hotel where Dad keeps a suite."

"I knew who she was." A kernel of guilt formed in his gut, but he didn't care. He really didn't. At least he told himself that. "But she didn't know me. She came on to me and I wanted her. I wasn't about to shut it all down to explain something that really didn't matter."

Michael groaned, a frustrated sound. "It mattered to her. Do you know why she left Interpol?"

He wasn't buying that argument. "I'm not her coworker. I'm nothing but handy cover. And I'm not using Nina. I'm trying to have a relationship with her. I can't explain it, Mike. I looked at her and I knew she was something special. I knew I had to get to know her. I still feel that way but times about a million. I can be good for her. I'm going to be good for her, but I need time with her, and I can't do that if she takes off for London the minute this job is over. That's exactly what she'll do if I don't give us a strong foundation for a relationship."

"All right, but you should understand that if the truth comes out, she might not be happy about it. Like I said, I like her for you." Michael put a hand on his shoulder. "I'll back off. Be careful out there and do what she tells you to. She's smart and she knows what she's doing."

JT hoped he knew what he was doing, too.

# Chapter Seven

JT hugged his mother on the porch. "Thanks for the party, Mom. I think it went a long way toward selling our cover."

His mother looked toward his truck where Nina sat in the passenger's seat.

It was past midnight and tomorrow would be a long day, but he found himself reluctant to leave. He wished they could stay here for a day or two and let his parents get to know Nina, let Nina get to know him and where he'd come from.

They were about to be thrown into the crucible, and he wasn't sure they were ready. By this time tomorrow they would be settling in at the retreat, getting ready for the welcome party. Nina would be working, and he was going to have to give her some space.

Until they went to bed at night. Then they'd agreed he could be in charge.

"Is it really a cover?" his mother asked. "I know you told me you're interested in her and we teased you a bit, but I watched you at dinner. You're half in love with that woman."

He might be more than half. "I like her a lot. This is more than some job for me, and I think she feels the same. We had a connection even before she knew we were going to work together. Now I just have to convince her that connection is real."

"Your cousin seems to think she's wonderful. Simon sang her praises to me. Even Chelsea likes her, and that's saying something. Chelsea doesn't like anyone. They were so sorry they couldn't be here tonight, but little Sophy has an ear infection."

He'd missed his cousin, but worried Si might have been in Mike's camp. Simon and his wife Chelsea no longer worked for McKay-Taggart, though their new company often worked with them. Simon's new job meant he hadn't had a chance to weigh in on whether JT was screwing up the world. "I'll check in on them when we get back. I should go since we've got a flight in the morning. I'll see you when we get back. Call me if anything changes with Dad."

Michael stepped up and held out a hand. "Hey, I'll be here. I'm taking a couple of days off from work. I'll stay out here with the old man, so you don't have to worry."

It would be a relief. Not that he didn't trust his mother. He simply didn't want her to be alone. That had been his place in the family for so long—the dutiful son, the one who always thought of the family and the business before himself. The one who hadn't had a real relationship in years because he hadn't found anyone he thought was perfect for the family and the business.

Fuck it. He didn't care if Nina fit in, though she likely would. He'd realized he'd looked for the "perfect" wife because he hadn't found the right one before. When the connection was right, perfection didn't mean a thing. All that mattered was being with her.

He shook his brother's hand. "Thank you. I'll concentrate on the mission."

Michael shook his hand and rolled his eyes. "Yeah, sure you will."

He stepped away. "You say that because you think I'm talking about the spy mission. I'm talking about my mission, brother, and I assure you I'm dedicated to that one."

He jogged down the steps where the truck and Nina were waiting for him.

His mission would be making her never want to leave him. Nina was his mission and he didn't intend to fail.

He slid into the cab and buckled his belt. The valet had the cab nice and toasty, though the weather was a bit chilly outside. "You ready? I called the hotel and they said everything's been delivered, including your new luggage. All you should have to do is pack."

"And go over a few things for the mission. The rest of the team is there, and I've got a call scheduled with them in the morning to ensure everything is running smoothly. I need to prepare for that, so I think I should stay in the guest room tonight."

She'd given up her room when they'd decided to spend time together. The suite had a second bedroom, but every night this week she'd slept in the master with him. He sighed and pulled the truck away from the house he'd called home all of his life. "So they scared you off?"

"No," Nina replied. "Your family is perfectly lovely, but the whole time I should have been watching our suspects, I was thinking about you. I was talking to your mother instead, or asking your father about you. It wasn't very professional of me."

"The mission hasn't started yet. I don't think it would have done much good to try to question Deanna, Patrick, and Jordy at a party where you're supposed to be getting to know everyone. I'm not especially close to them, so it made sense you would talk to my family." He could salvage this. "You looked like a woman getting to know her fiancé's family. That's a good thing."

"It would be if I'd meant to do it, but I didn't. I found myself falling into conversation and forgetting all about what I was actually there to do." She kept her eyes on the road ahead of them. "This mission is more important than our relationship."

"It doesn't have to be."

"This is my job and it's all I have. It has to be more important."

He could argue with her, but now wasn't the time. They had five days on the island ahead of them, and despite what she was obviously planning, she would spend most of that time with him. "So you've decided we shouldn't sleep together."

She turned in her seat. "I've decided we need to understand that this is a sexual relationship and it can't last. I have to go back to London, and you'll do your thing. Maybe we could see each other when we can, but you need a different type of woman."

"What does that mean?"

"It means I saw your life tonight and I don't see where I would fit. Your mother is a very traditional wife."

That showed what she knew. "My mother once shot up a CIA team with tranquilizers so my cousin and his future wife could sneak away from them."

Nina finally looked his way, and the smile that slid across her face was so brilliant it lit up the night. "She did what?"

He was glad he had a few stories to tell her, too. "It was back when my brother had first joined the CIA unit. They all came out here and they were trying their damnedest to recruit Chelsea. Simon didn't want her to join the Agency."

"Shouldn't it have been her choice?" Nina asked in that way that let him know there was only one answer.

Except he knew the truth. He'd been there. "Ten was blackmailing her."

"Ah, that sounds like the Agency. So your mother decided to shoot everyone?"

It was so good to hear the amusement in her voice. "That was actually my plan. See, we have lots of tranq darts because this is a ranch and we don't always want to kill an animal that's gone a little rogue. But I couldn't do it on my own, and my dad has an all-American respect for government employees. I do not. Oh, I respect the ones who deserve it, but Ten Smith was wrong. So I didn't have a problem teaming up with my surprisingly-accurate-when-she-shoots momma. It gave Si a chance to make his case to the woman of his dreams. Now the woman of his dreams was Chelsea Denisovitch."

Nina laughed at that. "He's got some interesting dreams. She was The Broker. Interpol had eyes on them. I know everyone wanted us to believe it was Charlotte, but I knew the truth."

"That's what I've figured out, too. But at the time all that mattered was Simon was in love with her and Ten had convinced her she needed to give it all up and work for him. I believe he'd promised he would solve all of Simon's problems if she would come work for him. I knew my cousin was in trouble and I wanted to give him a shot at talking to her. So Momma and I very quietly took out a CIA special ops team."

He made it to the end of the long drive to the farm road that would take them to the highway. From there they would pass Fort Worth and the suburbs and make their way back into Dallas.

Where apparently he would sleep alone tonight.

"That was quite brave of you. Do you know what Ten could have done?" Nina asked.

He hadn't really thought about it at the time. "It was important. I had to gamble that he needed my help more than he wanted revenge. Like I've mentioned before, the Agency has used Malone Oil more than once. International companies can give an operative excellent cover."

"And it didn't hurt that he wanted Michael on the team." She sat back and seemed to relax as they started down the long highway.

"No, it didn't."

"Is it odd to be a twin?"

He took it as a good sign. She was asking him something personal. "Not to me, but then I've had a twin since I was conceived. He's always been there."

"And then he wasn't."

"And then he wasn't." He didn't talk about this much because no one ever asked him. "He didn't even tell me he was going into the Navy. We graduated and I thought we would take a month off and travel some, but he was on his way to Great Lakes the day after."

"He didn't tell you?" The question was quiet but conveyed a sense of shock.

"He left me a note," JT admitted. "I suppose he didn't want me to try to talk him out of it. Or he didn't want to talk about it at all. He'd made his decision."

She was silent for a moment before she asked her next question. "Are you the one who always compromises?"

"I don't think Mike would put it that way. I think he believes the first twenty years of his life were a compromise. I don't know. I was happy."

"Because of Dana?"

She'd learned a lot about him. She obviously hadn't been lying when she'd said she'd spent her time thinking of him. Still, he wasn't sure he wanted to talk about this.

"It's all right," she said as though she'd read his mind. "You don't have to say anything."

But shouldn't he want to have someone to talk to? He'd made a friend a while back. Jared Johns. They'd gotten pretty close. He and his new wife Sarah had moved to California, and they were waiting on their first baby, so they talked less now. He didn't blame the guy, but for a moment it had been good to have a friend. He was friendly with guys on the rigs, but he never stayed long enough, and he was the boss. He had some guys he'd hung out with in college, but they were all getting married and having kids.

"Dana was the daughter of my father's best friend. We grew up together. Our parents always joked that she would marry one of us—either me or Mike, but everyone knew it would be me." His heart hurt whenever he thought of Dana. "I don't know. She was always there, too."

"And then she wasn't," Nina said gravelly.

"And then she wasn't."

"A lot of people have left you."

"Only the most important ones." He'd never thought about it this way. "Don't think I'm feeling sorry for myself. I've had a good life. But I miss them. I didn't love her. Not the way I was supposed to. Maybe I would have if she'd chosen me. I would have married her. I would have gotten out of college and married Dana and taken my place in the company. Is that wrong? That I'm the one who accepted the place my parents made for me?"

"It's not wrong to want something. It's wrong to reject something simply because your parents wanted it for you. The same way it's not wrong to reject something you truly don't want. From what I learned about you and your brother this evening I don't think either of you fall into those categories."

They didn't. When he looked back on it, he realized the signs of his brother's unhappiness had been there. He'd simply ignored them. "I loved this business for as long as I'm able to remember. I wanted to do this. I wanted to own Malone Oil. As I got older I wanted to learn all the ways I can take us from Malone Oil to Malone Energy. I've got my fingers in a lot of sustainable pies right now. This is my dream. But Mike never wanted what I wanted, and we've never recovered from him walking away. I forgave him a long time ago, but we're still out of synch. He still seems closer to his friends. That's the sad thing. I never found a person who could replace him, but he's replaced me several times over."

"He hasn't replaced you. He can't do that." Her voice had gone warm and sympathetic. "But he hasn't forgiven himself, and you can't make him. I assure you that forgiveness is harder than you think. I should know."

"What haven't you forgiven yourself for? The guy who tricked you?" He'd talked to a couple of her coworkers tonight and he'd come to realize so much of her reluctance came from that asshole.

"His name was Roger," she began slowly. "We were partners for two years before I ever agreed to go out with him. I thought I was being careful. I think he knew how to play me. I wasn't attracted to him at first. But it's a lonely job. It's hard because you can't talk about it."

"I can imagine. He was the only one who understood what it is to do what you do. Or what you did. You don't have the same boundaries with this job, right?"

"No. I can talk about this job for the most part. Not the particular one we're about to do since we're technically working with the Agency," she allowed. "But the day-to-day stuff isn't confidential. Also, we're one big team. It's like a big family, and that has to do with the unique culture of the job."

He thought he knew what she was talking about. He kept his eyes on the road, but his mind was entirely on her. His brother had talked about The Garden and how different it was from Sanctum. It had been the home to all of the Lost Boys until recently when they'd been able to finally get their lives back. "You all live in the same building, right? And the club you play at is there, too."

"Most of us live there and yes, the ground floor of the building is the club. It's truly beautiful. It should be weird to work and live and play in the same place, but Damon's done an excellent job of making the spaces very separate. I think in the beginning Damon had this huge building and he didn't want to be all alone in it. When he transitioned from MI6 to working with Tag, it made sense to let some of his employees live in the flats."

"I know a little about that. When you work on a rig, you sleep, work, eat all in the same spaces for months at a time. It can build a strong team. It can also make you want to murder some of the fuckers." At first those rigs had given him an odd sense of freedom. He still felt it a bit, though the older he got the more stability he wanted.

"It's not so bad where we are. There's more room, I suspect, and the accommodations are more luxurious," she said with a chuckle. "My flat is far larger than my place in Lyon was. It's also nice to have someone to eat dinner with. Someone's always on their own and looking for company. At least they used to be."

"Things are changing?" He knew how that felt. When everyone else was getting their lives in order and pairing off and starting families, it could make a man feel like he was getting left behind.

"Aren't they always?" she asked with a wistful air. "Damon and Penny split their time between The Garden and their home in the countryside. They're about to have another baby. I suspect Penny will start staying out there quite a bit. My friend Hayley and her husband Nick recently had a little girl. They're looking for a place close to The Garden. Last week Owen and Rebecca announced they're pregnant, too. There aren't many singletons left in our group. Certainly not since the lads got their freedom back. Is it odd to be surrounded by these lovely people who treat you like family and still feel so outside? Like they've all invited me in, but I can't quite make it through the door."

"Why do you think that is? You said you weren't close to your sister. How about your parents?" He was going to keep her talking. He hated the wistfulness in her tone, like she wanted something so badly but couldn't reach out and grab it. He understood that, too.

She thought about it for a moment before answering. "My family wasn't like yours. My dad was pretty distant, and I don't think my mum ever really understood me. She was closer to my sister, who definitely never understood me."

"My brother...I thought he did," he admitted. "And maybe he did, but I didn't try enough to understand him. I'm fully aware there's blame in here for me. I thought because I was happy that he was, too. The whole twin psychic connection thing might be true for some, but not me and Mike. Did you only have the one sister?"

She nodded. "Yes. She's five years younger than I am. It should have made us close, but we never were. We never had that sibling relationship for some reason. I think we were just far enough apart that we didn't spend much time together."

"You wouldn't have been in the same schools. Mike and I were obviously always in the same class."

"Yes, we just missed each other, though I don't know if it would have mattered. We're quite different personality-wise and in what we want out of life," she said. "It was like we lived in the same house but completely different lives. And then we didn't live in the same house at all. After university I lived in France for a long time, and it was a demanding job. At least that's what I told myself. My parents divorced while I was in my teens, and my father got remarried very quickly. His new wife didn't want to have anything to do with us, so he didn't. I haven't seen my father in ten years. When I moved back to London I spent a bit of time with my mum, but I found I couldn't take the comparisons to my sister's perfect life."

"I doubt it's perfect."

"It looks that way on social media, and that's all that matters to my mum and sister." She was quiet for a moment. "I'm surprised you're not on social media more often."

"I can't stand it. Don't get me wrong, I've got a page to keep up with people I was friendly with in high school and college, but I almost never post. Half the time I don't have Internet access. I don't think anyone wants to see pics of me sweaty and covered in grease. That's pretty much my existence when I'm on a rig." He realized he wasn't even doing the speed limit, which here was seventy-five. He was trying to drag out their time together. It wasn't fair to her since they had to be up and on a plane in the morning, and she would likely stay up doing her prep work. He forced himself to ramp up the speed.

Nina snorted, an oddly sweet sound. "Sure. The Internet would hate pictures of your sweaty muscles. Everyone would be disgusted. I bet we could make a calendar of you on oil rigs and it would sell like crazy."

"Then I could give the profits to green causes and make my dad insane." He wouldn't mind as long as she was his photographer.

"You really are exploring sustainable energy?"

"Absolutely," he replied, though he needed to be completely honest with her. He wasn't some vegan, spare-the-earth type. He had practical reasons for what he was doing. "I'm working with the king of Loa Mali. Don't think I'm doing it to save the earth or anything, though. I'm doing it because if I don't someone else will, and they'll be the ones making money off it. Though a cleaner earth wouldn't be so bad. I like clean air as much as the next guy. Maybe more since I grew up with so much of it."

She relaxed back. "I liked your family quite a bit. They're oddly down to earth for a group of billionaires."

"That's my mom and dad. I think it's because the ranch has always been so important. The ranch is how the Malones originally made our money, so even though it isn't important to us financially now, it is the bedrock of who we are. And if it means anything, they liked you, too. My mother in particular, and she's the one who can be hard to convince." He stared out at the twin lights illuminating the road in front of him. This was a lonely two-lane road that led to the wider highway. He glanced in the rearview out of habit. There wasn't a moon to illuminate the fields around him, but he would have sworn he could see a shadow behind him, just on the edge of the light from the back of the truck.

Was someone following them? He felt every muscle tense. Something was about to happen. Something wasn't right.

"What's going on?" Nina had sat right back up and she was looking his way now, a concerned expression on her face.

"I don't know." He looked in the rearview mirror, trying to catch that glimpse again. Something lurked right outside his vision. He was almost sure of it. "I'm probably being paranoid."

He didn't think so, but he didn't trust his own instincts when it came to this. He'd spent the whole evening thinking someone was watching him. He'd sat at dinner and talked to people he'd known for years, wondering the whole time if he or she was the one intent on betraying the company.

Nina turned in her seat. "You think someone's following us?"

He didn't want to scare her. Damn it. Maybe his brother was right about a few things. She needed to know what he'd seen. Or not seen. "I thought I caught sight of a shadow. I don't know. It's really dark, and this kind of darkness can play tricks on a person."

They were far enough from the ranch that there was zero light that didn't come from his headlights or the stars above them. The Malones owned all this land and it wasn't developed. He could remember all the times he and his brother and their friends would camp out and stare up at the stars.

It was a new moon, and now all he could see were shadows.

"I don't see anything," Nina said, looking in her passenger-side mirror. "No. There it is. JT, I need you to stay calm."

That was the moment he felt the whole truck jolt forward as something hit them hard from behind. It took everything he had to go against his instinct, which was to slow down and pull over. He couldn't do that. This wasn't some drunk asshole who'd forgotten to turn on his lights.

His heart rate jumped because there was zero way that hit had been an accident. Someone had followed them and was purposefully trying to run them off the road.

Whoever was in that vehicle would likely then make sure he or she finished them off.

Someone was trying to kill him.

He put the pedal to the metal. "We're not far from the main highway. We won't be alone there."

He had to keep them on the road. He hadn't asked Nina if she was carrying. He wasn't sure if it would matter at all if he lost control. They could be sitting ducks.

"Can you see a license plate?" Nina's voice was perfectly calm. She twisted in her seat again, trying to look behind them.

He could barely see the road in front of him. He looked in the rearview, but the shark that was following them had gone underwater again. He knew the predator was there, waiting to take another bite. But he couldn't see past the darkness. "It's too dark."

The truck was hit again, jerking him forward. He was already pushing eighty. The road on either side sloped off here. He had to be very careful or they would roll and end up like a turtle on its back.

He had to be careful or he could kill Nina. Someone was trying to kill him, and they could get Nina instead.

His fingers tightened around the steering wheel. Could he outrun the asshole? Or would more speed make things worse? He didn't see a way to ditch the other truck until they made it to the main highway. There were no side roads to disappear down. There were no handy cops working the night shift who might see them go by and join in the chase.

They were alone, and Nina's life was in his hands.

"Try to keep things steady," Nina was saying, and she had something in her hand. "I'm going to see if I can get a picture of the car."

"What?" He took his eyes off the road for a moment and watched in horror as she unbuckled her belt and lowered the back of her seat so she could twist around fully.

"I want to see if I can get a picture." She sounded like nothing was wrong at all. "This phone has an excellent camera and it's got a flash. It's dark enough out here that the light might surprise the bugger. Get ready. He's closing in again."

JT braced as the truck was bumped again. "You need to be in your damn seatbelt."

If he lost control, she could get thrown out the front windshield, and at these speeds she wouldn't survive it. His heart threatened to pound out of his chest at the thought of what could happen to her.

"Just a sec." She cursed under her breath as she was jostled again. Her shoulder hit him hard. "Sorry."

He managed to stay in his lane. "I think you need to get back in your seat."

She was still moving, her back now somehow to him. "How far did you say we are from the highway? I bet he'll break off there. He won't want to get caught on traffic cameras."

"Two miles." The way he was going it wouldn't take more than a minute or two to get there. "This road flows into that one. It's a yield. No hard stop."

"Excellent. Just keep her on the road for me. I don't know how he's going to react to this."

There was a flash of light and then he heard brakes squealing.

"Got him." Nina was smiling as she popped back into her seat and brought it to its original position.

"Put the belt on," he managed to bite out.

She did as he asked. "Fine, but I think we're all right now. Even if he only stops for a moment, we'll lose him from here. Now we see if I got a face. Or a plate."

In his rearview, he saw red lights come on and then race away. "He made a U-turn. He's driving away."

"Excellent," she said, looking down at her phone. "Tech might be able to get something off this."

"That was dangerous as hell," he said, starting to breathe again.

"It was fine," she replied, not looking up from her phone. She'd started typing. "I'm in my belt now and the bad guy's going the other way. You did a great job. You kept us on the road, and I might be able to figure out who that was."

"We nearly died."

"But we didn't and now everything's fine." She finally looked up. "Ian's still awake. He's going to meet us at the hotel and hopefully he'll have some news for us."

Excellent. His night was far from over.

# Chapter Eight

"The truck is stolen, but then we really should have expected that especially if we're dealing with a pro." Ian Taggart paced the big suite, still dressed in the button-down and slacks he'd worn to the party. "According to the police report, it went missing earlier this evening. I had Derek contact the local police. They believe it was someone who stole it and was driving drunk. It'll get buried really fast. You two did a good job talking to them. I don't think they'll follow up."

"Adam will see if he can do anything with facial recognition." Alex had been waiting with Ian when JT had handed off his truck to the valet downstairs, who hadn't said a thing about the dents and deep gouges to the back. "The police out in Parker County have already found the vehicle. We'll let you know if they find any prints, but I suspect they won't."

Nina had been relieved to have a distraction since the hour-long drive to Dallas had been almost completely silent.

Silent, and not comfortable. She could practically hear the wheels in JT's head grinding, and they weren't coming up with anything Nina thought they should. She was afraid she was about to be introduced to the JT who'd lost his closest female friend. She understood, but she couldn't allow it to derail the mission, and she worried that's exactly what JT would try to do.

"I'm sorry I couldn't get a better shot of him. My impression from the brief glimpse I got was of a male. Not that it tells us anything. I would assume this person was hired." She stood by the window where only days ago she'd been with JT, letting the night cradle them, pretending nothing in the world could get to them.

She'd known it was a pretty lie even before she'd realized who her new lover was. She'd known her time with him was probably short.

They'd stolen a few days, but now she wondered if it was coming to an abrupt end. She was surprised at how far she might be willing to go to not allow that to happen.

JT stood across the room from her, still quiet, but she could sense the boiling emotions threatening to bubble over. His tension was etched in the hard line of his expression. He might have faced down pirates before and lots of scary situations, but she doubted he'd done it when he was with someone he deeply cared about. It was a different kind of anxiety, and she didn't think he was handling it well.

"I'm happy you thought to try to get us a picture of the asshole at all. That was quick thinking," Tag said. "Also it gave me and Alex the rest of the night off. We were pulling into Alex's driveway to drop them off when we got the call."

Alex grinned. "I've never seen Big Tag move so fast. Apparently the sitter called and told Charlotte that Travis woke up and won't go back to sleep."

"Charlie tried to cover it up, but I could hear that kid wailing in the background," Big Tag acknowledged. "Before you start writing the *Am I the Asshole* post, I had him all last weekend while Charlie and Chelsea did a sisters thing that I pray was really about massages and mani pedis, because their sister time used to be spent taking over small countries."

"And I was just making sure Ian doesn't get in trouble," Alex added. "It has nothing to do with the fact that we'll now have to stay over here and make sure no one tries to kill JT again. Nothing to do with the fact that I can sleep in instead of waking up to a dirty diaper in the face because Eve brings the baby into bed with us thinking she'll be able to sleep a little longer. Vivian never sticks her stinky diaper in her momma's face. No. It is always mine."

"Hey, when you and Theo figure out how to breastfeed, that can change for you," Tag snarked. "But Alex is right. We're going to bed down here and make sure everything goes smoothly. There's room service, right? I'm sure this place has killer room service, and I don't have to fight the girls for pancakes. They're surprisingly sneaky when it comes to food hoarding. They do not mind licking things."

Alex had gotten rid of his tie the minute they'd walked upstairs. "And hey, we'll need to make sure you two make it to the airport. Are you sure they don't need a bodyguard, because I could use a tan."

"Nah, we need to play this off like they're not worried," Big Tag said. "We're going with the police line that it was a drunk driver. We can't let anyone know you're worried someone's trying to kill you."

"Maybe we should talk to the police here in Dallas about the whole case." JT finally spoke, the words sounding grim coming out of his mouth. He leaned against the pool table. "Maybe it's time we bring the authorities in."

She shook her head. "That's not a good idea. What can the police do? We filed the accident report because that's a thing people do. If anyone goes looking for it, they'll find a report that we were hit. But that's why we didn't tell them what we suspected. We can't open that door. We're leaving tomorrow. The most they can do is exactly what Adam will do, and he's got better equipment."

"So much better," Alex agreed. "Also, calling in the cops would probably be akin to calling in the press. The minute a reporter gets a whiff that a Malone heir might be the target of an assassin, that story goes everywhere and then we scare off our spy."

"Maybe that's a good thing," JT said. "We scare off the spy and then we've got more time to figure out who killed my friend. That should lead us to the spy."

"The more likely outcome is the spy simply changes the time and place for the drop-off," she pointed out calmly. "We know who the actual spy is. We don't know who is working for you. This is our best shot at figuring out who your mole is."

He was quiet for a moment, but his head came up and a steely glint hit his eyes. "You're right. This is all about my company. I get to make the calls here. I say I don't care what happens to that tech."

Big Tag turned JT's way, his brows drawn together in obvious consternation. "What are you talking about? You do know how much money you stand to lose if someone else gets this tech before the patent goes through? Hell, even with the patent it can be hard to quash outside of the US and Europe."

"Not to mention the fact that we don't know what North Korea will do with that tech," Alex pointed out. "I know it seems like the only applications are in petroleum and gas, but a material that flexible could easily be used on warheads. From what I've read you've managed to create a new material that doesn't corrode the way some of the plastics we use now do. That's very important, JT."

JT's head shook. "Bill was the one who developed the actual material.

I gave him my ideas on what we need, especially for deep-sea drilling. I did a lot of the testing, but he's the smart one. The new material will ensure fewer leaks and keep the ocean cleaner. It should do the same thing for pipelines to ensure we don't pollute ground water."

"Yes, and I assure you someone will find a way to take that revolutionary thing you've helped create and pervert it," Tag said. "I've seen it a million times. We just managed to get a bunch of guys back on track after someone fucked up a medical breakthrough that should have been used for good."

"What's going on, JT?" Alex studied him for a moment. "You're not one to panic. When I realized you were going in instead of your father, I actually was happy about it. Your dad doesn't take anything very seriously, but you understand what's on the line. So why are you hesitating now?"

There was a long pause, and she realized the time where her boss didn't have to know she'd slept with the client was at an end. "He's worried about me."

Tag snorted. "Worried about you?" He gave JT a shake of his head. "I know she looks all soft and sweet, but Nina's solid, man. She might wear frilly dresses, but they hide a multitude of weapons she's incredibly accurate with. I applaud my sisters for putting those skirts to use. Do you know how hard it is to hide a knife on my thigh? I mean I can get it up there, but getting that fucker out is hell. And her getting a halfway decent photo of the dude trying to run you off the road? Pure gold. That's why I hired her. Cool as a cucumber."

"Damon actually hired me," she said, hoping maybe they would leave it at this. If they thought JT was merely upset that any woman had been put in danger, they might still come out of it with their secret intact. For a little while.

"She could have died." JT's jaw had tightened stubbornly. "She took her damn seatbelt off. When I was doing a hundred miles an hour."

"That's how she got the picture," Tag replied as though it should have been plain.

Alex seemed a bit more sympathetic to JT's problems. "I know it seemed reckless, but Nina knew what she was doing. I would have probably taken the same chance if I'd thought to. Not only does it give us a shot at figuring out if this was one of your employees or someone he or she hired, it also scared the asshole off. She might have saved you a lot more damage."

"Or I could have lost control of the damn truck and she could have died," JT insisted.

"But I didn't and everything is fine." She wished now they didn't have company because she needed to calm him down. She knew she'd said she would go to the guest room, but he needed her.

"You could have died." He shook his head. "No. This whole retreat is off. I'll call and make an excuse, but I'm not putting her in danger like this. It was one thing when I thought all she had to do was watch for the drop to happen, but no. Someone tried to kill me tonight. I'm not putting her in front of me like that."

"It's her job. It's literally her job to take a bullet if she has to. She did it really well last time. Didn't even die," Tag joked.

She appreciated the fact that Tag would never treat her any differently than a male operative working the same job. He would be sarcastic and he would give her all the backup she would need. He would also be absolutely certain she could do the job or he wouldn't have assigned it to her. "I don't know, boss. Given the two choices, I might have drank the roofied tea instead. Leaves less of a scar."

"That's how you got that scar?" JT asked. "I knew that was a bullet wound."

A long sigh came from Tag, and his stare went right for her. "Seriously? I thought you were my smart one."

Well, there went the secret. "Guess not."

Alex looked back and forth between her and Tag as though he didn't quite understand. "What? I think Nina's super smart."

"Not when it comes to fucking the client," Tag replied with another sigh. "And apparently making the client so happy while she's fucking him that he can't stand the thought of losing her. I will admit, though, that you are good at hiding that shit, Blunt. I picked up on him sniffing around you, but not that he'd already had a taste."

"Hey," JT said, suddenly standing tall.

It was obvious her billionaire had far too much stimulation for one day. "JT, he's not wrong, and sarcasm is his love language."

"He doesn't have to talk about you like that." JT's voice had gone dangerously low.

"He doesn't mean anything by it," she tried to explain.

"Stand down, Malone. I'm not impugning your lady's honor or anything." Tag didn't look worried about the potential for JT's anger. "I didn't know she was your lady. Normally I have an excellent radar that warns me when my employees are boffing the clients. Like I said, Nina's really good at covering."

Alex had folded his arms over his muscular chest. "Yeah, Ian's excellent at figuring out who's doing who. I mean who is having what is obviously a deep and meaningful relationship with another person involved in a mission."

Alex wasn't bad at snark himself.

It was time to come clean. "Ian, Mr. Malone and I met in the bar before the job started. We didn't realize who the other was, and one thing led to another. I assure you our physical relationship won't affect the mission."

"It's affecting the mission now," Ian replied.

"I think I should have some say in how this goes." JT wasn't giving up.

Her heart sank. She knew what he was doing, knew why he was doing it, but this was her job. He'd promised her he understood, and the first time she was in danger, he was playing the white knight and not letting her do what she needed to do. Now that she didn't have to hide their relationship, she could at least try to save the situation the only way she knew how. "I think JT and I should talk about this privately."

JT stared at her. "There's nothing to talk about. I can't believe you did that. I can't believe you put yourself in that position."

It had been a risk but a calculated one. "You were handling the situation well. I thought about it and decided to try to get us an edge. You knew the area. You knew your truck. I trusted that you could keep us on the road."

JT's eyes had narrowed. "But what if I hadn't? You could have gone through the windshield. Hell, the way you were sitting, you could have gone all the way through the back of the truck. You wouldn't have survived that. I do know that road. I know exactly how dangerous it is. Animals cross there all the time, and they pop out of nowhere. Anything could have happened."

He was definitely feeling the aftereffects of adrenaline. Perhaps if they'd been more secure in their relationship, he would have yelled at her in the truck and they wouldn't be doing this in front of her bosses. She truly understood why he was upset. He wasn't a trained operative. He wasn't used to being in danger. He definitely wasn't used to the panic that could come with some of the situations she'd been put in. She'd learned how to stay calm, though the instinct to panic had been there. It had been all about him. "I was worried about you too, but we had to do our best given the situation, and we did."

"From what I can tell, you two made a great team." Tag was watching them as though trying to figure out how to handle the client.

"Well, I'm not putting my teammate in more danger," JT insisted. "The mission is off."

"You can't call it off. I know tonight was disturbing, but we don't get to walk away from this. We're dealing with the Agency. This mission is about far more than Malone Oil." She needed to get through to him. She crossed the space between them and took his hand in hers. "I understand exactly what you're feeling, but you can't make big decisions right now. You need to sleep on it, and I think you'll find things are different in the morning. You'll be able to see the situation with more clarity."

He stared down into her eyes. "You think I'll care less about what happens to you in the morning? Because I assure you I won't. I'll still want you safe."

He really was heartbreakingly handsome. She wanted nothing more than to brush back that dark lock that tumbled over his forehead and made him look younger than he really was. She wanted to take him to bed and make him forget they'd been in danger at all. "No, I think time gives us the distance we need to properly assess. Right now you're too close to the fear to understand how well the encounter went. You did a magnificent job. You did everything I needed you to do. I was perfectly happy going into this job with you as my partner before, and the way you handled that truck and the ride back reinforced that belief."

His shoulders relaxed, and she almost thought she had him.

"I can't put you in that position again," he said grimly.

"And that is why it's a bad idea to get involved with the client." Tag's voice was every bit as somber.

Irritation began to war with sympathy. She had to find a way to get him to understand. "JT, this is my job and I'm good at it. You need to listen to me. Imagine me trying to tell you how to work a rig. Or explain engineering to you."

He shook his head. "It's not the same. I get that you have a dangerous job, but I shouldn't make it more dangerous. That doesn't mean I have to put you in harm's way. I think what you should do is take a couple of weeks off and spend them here with me. You don't have to do this job at all. You don't need it. I can find something else for you."

Alex stood up. "Maybe we should leave them alone for a while."

"And miss the show?" Tag asked.

She turned on her boss. "I think I can handle this."

"I'm sorry, but I don't think you can, and I can't leave until we figure out what we're going to do," Tag announced with a sad shake of his head. "We don't have time for you to bring him around. My contract is with Malone Oil, not JT's dick. Don't look at me like that, man. That's exactly what you're thinking with, and I'm not judging you for it. You're in deep with a girl. That's when your dick takes over. Unfortunately, the Agency isn't going to wait for Nina to convince you she's not going to wither and die without a male hand guiding her."

"That isn't what I said." JT was staring at Tag like he might try to take the big guy on.

"I assure you that's what she heard," Tag countered. "You're making a bad play and it won't work."

She wasn't sure exactly what she was hearing beyond JT's fear. It had been a rough night for him, and if she had any choice at all, she wouldn't push him. She would go to bed with him and they could talk this out in the morning. She'd made the decision to spend the night alone, but she hadn't been unaffected by what had happened. She could have lost him, and in the face of that, it seemed silly to need time alone. They needed some time together if they were going to see if this had any chance of working. Unfortunately, time wasn't on their side, and she had to find a way to make JT see that. "We're not sure what the Agency will do. That's what Tag is talking about. We have a duty to your company to keep this operation in our hands. If we pull out, the Agency won't stop. Right now they're satisfied we can handle things, but they believe this technology is important. They do not want it in the wrong hands. Malone Oil could find itself in a bad place if McKay-Taggart isn't handling this mission."

"*Will* find themselves in a bad position," Tag corrected. "There's no question about that."

"I agree." Alex settled in as though he knew they weren't going to be able to give them the privacy they needed.

She shoved her frustration down. "Let's go somewhere and talk about this. We need it settled because we're supposed to get on a plane tomorrow and we're supposed to be engaged. We can't fight with each other and you can't be tense. They will pick up on it and change their plans. That can't happen. We've got one shot at this and if we screw up, that prototype will be on the way to North Korea."

JT seemed to think about it, but the minute she saw the stubborn glint in his eyes, she knew all her patience was going to be for nothing.

"I'll say we broke up. There are already people in place. There are several McKay-Taggart employees already down there on the island. They can do the job. Hutch and Sandra are there, right? And the CIA guy is there. I don't understand why we need Nina."

And she was done explaining things to him. It was obvious he wasn't going to listen and that his fear was worth far more to him than she was. She had to keep a tight rein on her emotions because she really wanted to lose her temper. Or cry. She wasn't sure if she would be crying because she was so angry with him or because he was marginalizing her. Maybe both. It didn't matter, though, because she would cling to what she always had—her work. It was time to stop worrying about JT and start doing her actual job. She turned to Tag. "I think we should call Michael in. With a haircut he looks exactly like JT, and I assume he knows something about the business."

"You fucking will not," JT shouted. He seemed to realize he'd raised his voice and he checked himself. "I'm sorry. I didn't mean to yell, but you're not sending my brother in."

She saw Tag start to address the situation, but this was hers to deal with and she wasn't hiding behind anyone. "Mr. Malone, I understand that you're used to being in control, but this is my mission and if you don't comply, I will be forced to have you taken into custody. At that point I will take your brother with me and we will complete our mission. It would be safer for all involved if you did what you promised to do, but make no mistake. I will be on that plane tomorrow with you or without you."

His stare threatened to burn a hole through her. "Your way or the highway, huh, Nina?"

She hated the fact that she had to fight back tears. "In this, yes it is. I believe we agreed to that when we began. When we realized the situation we were in, I agreed to try a relationship with you only because you agreed that I was in charge of the mission. You should understand I never would have touched you if I had realized who you were for this very reason."

His expression had softened and there was a clear look of panic on his face, as though he finally realized he'd gone way too far. "Hey, I wasn't pushing you away. Damn it, Nina, I'm doing this to protect you."

Tag's face had darkened, the first time during any of this that she'd been worried about what her boss would do. "Did he tell you he didn't know who you were that first night?"

"He didn't." She didn't want to explain this, but she owed her boss something. "I still thought I was going in with his father, and I honestly hadn't studied up on the rest of the family. I knew David Malone had two sons and Michael worked with the Dallas team, but I hadn't met Michael. I probably should have read a dossier on him when I agreed to the mission. I have now."

"Why would you?" Tag countered. "He wasn't part of the mission. I'm not accusing you of anything. You were doing your job and you had every right to sit in a bar when you weren't working and hook up with whoever you liked. But I assure you JT knew exactly who you were. My assistant even told him where you were staying. I asked Genny to bring him up to speed because I knew we didn't have much time. She sent JT a dossier on you. I waited to send you his until I knew he was going to do the job. You'd had a long flight. I assumed you would be asleep, which is why you didn't get that info until the morning. But he knew."

He couldn't have. "I only gave him my first name. I came on to him."

"I wanted to talk to you," JT said, not quite meeting her gaze. "It had been a rough day and I needed to meet you. And then you were sitting in the bar and you were so beautiful."

Her stomach sank. "You knew who I was when I hit on you."

It wasn't a question. It was blatantly obvious she'd been had. He'd known exactly who she was and he'd lied to her.

It was the one thing she'd asked him not to do. Well, that and treat her less than she was.

"I knew we had chemistry, and you wouldn't have given us a chance if you'd known," he said quickly. "Nina, baby, you hit me like lightning, and I know you felt the same way. The job didn't matter."

"It mattered to me." She needed to get out of here. She knew it wasn't professional, but she had to get away from him, had to think her way through this.

It was happening again. She was trading her job, her reputation, for some good sex and a modicum of affection.

She wasn't ever going to learn.

"Ian, I'm going to do some prep work and write up a report of my observations of our suspects. Should I do that while I'm watching the client or were you and Alex serious about staying here?" She didn't even look JT's way.

"I think that's an excellent idea. We should all get some sleep. I'll let Michael know to be on standby," Ian replied. "We'll stay here but you have to stay here, too. I'd love to get you another room or let you go to the office, but we don't know who's watching."

She wanted to be away from JT, wanted some time alone to mourn what had just happened, but she understood what Ian was saying.

She almost prayed they ended up taking Michael with them. If they managed to convince JT to go through with the mission, she would have to hold hands with him and look like they were in love.

It would be torture.

"I'll take the smaller bedroom." At least they were in a ridiculously large suite and she had options.

"You can have the master," JT replied.

"Thank you." She turned away because she wasn't about to argue.

\* \* \* \*

JT stared out over the lights of Dallas and tried to find any beauty at all in them. It was three in the morning and he hadn't found a second of peace since that moment when he'd realized someone was trying to kill him and that person might get Nina instead. It was hard to believe he'd stood in this same spot mere days before and thought it was the most beautiful place in the world. But then Nina had been here with him.

"I would tell you to move away from the exposed window anyone could snipe you from, but I suspect you wouldn't hate that at this point," a familiar voice said.

He wished the voice wasn't so familiar but was at least relieved it wasn't Tag. He turned from the floor-to-ceiling windows with a sigh and took in Alex McKay, who was down to his slacks, undershirt, and socks. The sight of McKay's gun in a shoulder holster reminded him why McKay was here, and it wasn't simply to avoid stinky diapers. "Sorry. I'll keep away from the window, though I don't see how anyone could get me this high."

McKay glanced out. "I've got four perches I could use, and then there are always helicopters, though those will give you a bit of a warning. You would be surprised how many people don't take a good warning though."

"Yeah, I got that." He crossed to the bar and poured himself a Scotch. It was his first since Nina had looked at him with wounded eyes. He'd forced himself to stay away from it because he'd needed to think. He was tired of thinking. Thinking got him nowhere. Thinking had left him with nowhere to sleep. "Tag kick you out of bed?"

McKay chuckled and sat down at the bar. "His snoring sure did. Let me tell you I do not miss having to share a room with the big bastard. When we first started the company years ago we did it on a shoestring budget and had to share hotel rooms, and they did not always have two beds. The funny thing is he's completely silent when we're on surveillance. I swear that man can sleep with his eyes open and not make a sound. But when he's comfortable, he can scare off an elephant. I don't know how Charlie does it."

"It's good that he's so comfortable. I could have been comfortable if he'd kept his mouth shut." Nina hadn't given up on him until Tag had outed his tiny omission of truth.

Alex slid him a sidelong glance. "I doubt that. I don't know what conversation you were having last night, but it was not going well."

"I could have saved it. I could have made her understand, but Tag had to open his mouth. I tell you I was disappointed. I kind of thought we were friendly. I didn't expect he would out me like that to Nina." It had bugged him all night. She never had to know how they'd met. It didn't change anything.

Alex chuckled and poured himself a couple of fingers of the excellent Scotch the hotel stocked for the Malones. "Oh, that didn't surprise me at all. Look, Ian's got a code and he's got a bunch of circles with which he applies that code. And he would blow a whole lot of that code up if he thinks a guy is fucking a woman over."

Then Tag didn't know him at all. "I am not trying to hurt Nina. I am trying to keep her safe."

"You started the relationship by lying to her. That was always going to come out. You've been lucky so far. I assure you at some point Genny would have asked Nina about you and it would have come out. But you can't expect Ian to pick you in this fight. She's his employee, and he takes that seriously. Also, I know Ian seems like he's all about protecting the women, but half the time he's got a woman watching his back. He's kind of surrounded himself with badass women, and he doesn't like it when they get marginalized."

What the hell was Alex talking about? "I wasn't marginalizing her. I was trying to put her first. That's what I don't get. I'm literally willing to give up millions of dollars so she can be safe and somehow I'm the bad guy."

This was what he'd been up thinking about all night. He had no idea how he'd been on the losing side of this fight. He was putting her first, putting her above money, the company, hell, according to Tag and Alex, he was putting her above the country. He didn't get what he'd done so wrong, why she'd looked at him like he'd torn her apart.

Alex's expression turned slightly sympathetic. "I wouldn't say bad guy exactly, but you're definitely the asshole. You've been around Nina for a week now. I would assume you've talked to her. Or have you just spent time in bed?"

He'd spent more time with her in the last week than he'd spent with anyone in years. "Of course I've talked to her. I've gotten to know a lot about her. You might think I'm an asshole, but I care about her. I care about her more than I would have expected. Hell, I've spent days trying to figure out how to keep her here with me after this mission thing is over."

"Then you should know about her last job."

He sighed in pure frustration. The last thing he wanted to talk about was the asshole who'd gotten her fired from Interpol. "I'm not using her. I'm not lying to her to try to get something out of her. I know I didn't tell her I knew who she was, but I saw her and I wanted her more than I've ever wanted a woman in my life. I asked myself why it mattered that we would be working together."

"Then shouldn't you have made that argument to her?" Alex asked.

He'd thought about this, too. "I didn't want to risk it."

Alex nodded as though that was exactly the answer he'd expected. "Then you lied to her because you wanted to manipulate her into doing something. Namely you."

"It's not the same."

Alex took a short drink and seemed to savor the Scotch. "Okay. Well, then you're in the right and she's overreacting."

JT sank onto the seat beside Alex. "That's not what I'm saying either."

"Then you should say what you mean to say."

Wasn't that the problem? "I don't know what I mean to say. I didn't want any of this to happen. I wanted to be with her. That was all."

"But her job is a big part of who she is," Alex pointed out. "This isn't an office job she chose because there wasn't anything else out there. She trained for this. She puts her heart and soul into this job, and she's had it all ripped away from her before."

"I wasn't trying to take her job away." But he could see how it might look that way from her perspective. "I was trying to keep her safe."

Alex put the drink down. "She's not safe. That's part of who she is, and you're rejecting that part of her. How would you respond to a girlfriend who attempted to talk your father out of sending you out to check on rigs?"

"That would be ridiculous." Half his job was making sure the rigs were properly working.

"Why? It's dangerous. It's precisely why you have security on every one of those rigs, and even then, bad shit still happens."

"Yeah, well I've never been shot." He winced. "But I have been in dangerous positions. Damn it. I didn't mean to make her feel like she's less. She's starting to be everything to me."

"Do you want my advice? From a man who lost his wife because he didn't understand or appreciate how strong she was? I ask because I really will back off if you don't want my opinion. Unlike Ian, who would just plow through." Alex got a whimsical smile on his face. "I often think he does that because he never really fucked up before. He can be that arrogant because he was mostly right."

"That's the not the way I heard it." JT had been told a lot of stories about Big Tag. "I heard he was a complete ass when his wife made it back to him."

That comment elicited a full belly laugh from Alex. "Yeah, he was, but that lasted a whole three days. She put him through hell for five years. When you really look at it, he blustered briefly, and there was never a question in my mind what the outcome would be because he loved her. Because I watched for years as he mourned her. I sometimes wonder if he gave in so quickly because he'd seen how badly I screwed up."

"You and Eve were divorced, right?" He'd heard a bit about it from his brother, but he knew far more about the younger guys Michael worked with on a regular basis. Not that they had a bunch of romantic entanglements. Well, Boomer had that sandwich he was in love with...

"For years." Alex's face lost the whimsical expression. "She was assaulted while I was working a case and I treated her like she was made of glass. I was so afraid she could get hurt again, that I would hurt her again."

"It's not the same."

"You keep saying that, but it is," Alex insisted. "I wanted to wrap her up and never let anyone touch her again. It hurt her. It killed my marriage the first time around. I often think the world would have been very different if Charlotte hadn't died. Faked her death. I wonder if I would have made the same choices with Ian and Charlotte as my guide. I've heard some stories about them before they got married. They got into some crazy stuff. One time apparently they were after the same guy, like assigned to assassinate the same dude."

"He was a mobster," a deep voice said. "She was assigned to kill him because he was going to turn on her syndicate. I was supposed to do it because he had killed an Agency operative and stolen valuable intel."

Alex looked up as Tag walked in. Unlike Alex, he'd shucked his clothes and wore one of the hotel's super-plush robes over what JT thought was likely his boxers. "I thought you would sleep."

"I did for a while," Tag said with a yawn. "Then I had a shitty dream and when I woke up I remembered there's Scotch. It's funny because I always think I'll sleep better alone, and then I never do. I get cold without her. Now you were telling the story of me and Charlie and Russian No Balls. I call him that because Charlie shot his balls off before she put two in his chest. That woman is so sexy when she's working."

"You let her take your job?" It seemed inconceivable since what he knew of Tag was that he was a control freak.

Tag grabbed a glass. "I sat my pretty ass on the bed and watched her do it. I ate some very delicious chocolates because we happened to be in Belgium, and I made sure she was totally loose. Being loose is important when you're sniping someone, and it's a totally different experience than when I did it in the Army. In the Army they shove you in camo, give you a couple of MREs you can't heat up, and tell you to lie in position for hours, sometimes days, at a time. That was not the way Charlie played it. No. She got a suite in the nicest hotel in Antwerp." Tag snorted. "Antwerp…"

Alex groaned. "God, it's like you're still twelve. How about we skip how you kept Charlotte loose and get on to why you let her take out the bad guy?"

"She won rock paper scissors dick," Tag replied. "Seriously, when you're playing that don't pick dick. Everything hurts dick. Despite what our culture says with all its man-up talk, dicks are seriously delicate. I should never have let her add that in. I thought dick could pee on paper, but she offered to paper cut my dick and I then handed that rifle over."

"Ian," Alex prompted.

Tag's lips curled up. "Fine. I let her do it because she's a better shot than me. I would let her do it today because she's still a better shot at that range. My wife is one of the best operatives I've ever worked with, and there's no one in the world I want watching my back more."

"Who would you take in if you couldn't take your wife?" Alex asked.

"I would take you, asshole," Tag shot back. "You're my best friend, and for some reason you still want me alive. Now if you and Charlie were out, I know exactly who I'm taking in and that's Erin. I'm stealing her from Li because she's smart and mean and doesn't pull her punches. I can't help the fact that some of my best employees are chicks. I didn't hire them for their coffee-making skills. I hired them because they're good at their jobs and they're committed to doing what's right. I've sent women into dangerous positions because they were my absolute best bet at getting a job done, and one day it will very likely be my daughters I send in. When they're ready I won't hesitate because I won't ever treat them differently than I would my son. I won't teach them they're less. If they decide they want to teach school or cut hair, then good for them. They'll give it their all, and I'll do my best to make sure they're safe. But my girls are probably going to follow in their momma's footsteps, and that means they'll throw themselves into the dangerous stuff because it's their calling. I take it this conversation is about how JT fucked up?"

"Yeah, he still doesn't understand," Alex replied.

He hated feeling like everyone thought he was an idiot. "Look, I took all those training classes at Sanctum. I thought we were supposed to protect our subs. I know she's not wearing my collar, but I want to work toward that."

Ian snorted. "I don't think Nina's going to be that kind of sub." He sighed and sat back. "I'm sorry. I shouldn't make fun of you. It's habit. You seem to have missed the part of class where we talk about there being no one way to have a D/s relationship. I think you'll find Nina's on the 'keep it to the club' level of submission. Have you not talked about this at all? About how you would behave out in the field?"

He felt himself flush. "I told her I would defer to her since she's the pro."

"And then the first chance you get you tell her you're in charge," Alex pointed out.

"Dick move," Ian said. "Remember when I told you dicks are delicate. Yep, you proved my point."

"Look, man, this would be a solid plan if Nina was your assistant," Alex said.

"The funny thing is I wouldn't even have thought of pulling Deanna out." It was a tough admission to make. "One of the things I like about her is how solid she is. She's rough and sometimes mean, but I don't have to worry about her being…fragile. I do treat Deanna like I would any other employee."

"Nina isn't fragile either, and I for one wish I was going on this op because at some point in time that assistant of yours is going to get on Nina's last nerve, and that's when the wrestling begins," Tag said. "Have the resort place handy women-sized vats of your favorite gelatin product around the grounds and let them go at it."

He seriously doubted Nina would lose her cool. Because she was a professional. Because she had a job to do and she took it seriously. "I don't think I can stand it if she gets hurt."

Tag took a drink and sat back. "Then you need to find a woman with a safer job." He was quiet for a moment and then all sarcasm had been purged from his voice. "Is this about Dana?"

JT took a long breath and let it out. "Maybe partly. It gets easier over the years, but then something will remind me that she's gone and I don't know where she is. After all this time, I know she's probably dead, but I wish I knew."

"Chelsea is heartsick that she can't find a trace of her," Alex said. "It was one of the reasons she left the Agency and started this company with Adam."

"But some people, despite all of our best efforts, are never found. We lose some, and that's the hardest part of this job. We don't always win, but we get up the next day and we strap on our armor and go back into the fight." Tag gestured toward the hall that led to the master bedroom. "That's what Nina does. You need to decide if that's what you want. I'm not saying you can't have an amazing partner if she doesn't also snipe the bad guys. Avery O'Donnell is one of the finest women I've ever met, and she knows to duck when the bullets fly. Her strength is different but no less powerful. Nina needs to do her job to feel whole and complete. She will also need a partner who trusts her enough, who loves her enough, to take those risks with her."

"And that might not be you," Alex said with nauseating sympathy. "You should think about it."

"I really do think Michael can do this." Tag's voice was soft, offering him a way out. "And he does need a haircut."

He shook his head and finally took a long swig of that Scotch. It burned down his throat. "No. I'm going in with her. I'm going to find a way to win her back."

Tag nodded as though he approved. "Excellent. Then you're going to need a plan. Now let me tell you exactly how I kept my Charlie loose for her mission."

Alex groaned and dropped his head down to the bar.

JT only half listened as Big Tag gave him way too much information. His mind was on the mission. His mission.

He was going to win her back. He had to because he'd realized nothing mattered more than Nina. Not even his fear of losing her.

# Chapter Nine

Nina looked out over the beautifully decorated lanai and wished she was in a good place with JT because this island was seriously romantic. But they weren't here for romance. He was holding court with a group from his leadership team and she'd spent the last few hours trying to get to a mental place where she could be cool and collected. It had been a full day since she'd learned he'd lied to her, and she wished that knowledge made him even a little bit less attractive. He was dressed in slacks and a white button-down sans tie for this welcome cocktail party. Before they'd come down, she'd been forced to watch him walk around without a shirt on as he'd listened to Deanna go over a seemingly endless list of notes she'd made concerning the cocktail party they were about to attend. JT's assistant hadn't cared that they'd been running late and he needed to get dressed. She'd simply followed him around the big suite while he'd changed and stood outside the bathroom door when he'd needed some privacy.

Now Deanna was the one standing beside him, a glass of wine in her hand because Nina couldn't make herself do her damn job.

"I give it a month and the English chick is back in London," a woman said to her right.

Nina went still. There was a large potted palm tree between her and whoever was talking. It concealed her and allowed her to listen in.

"I don't know. I think she's pretty," another feminine voice said. "She actually reminds me a little of Ava Malone."

"Only because she's British," the first woman argued. "She definitely doesn't have Ava's instincts. If someone like Deanna got her claws into David Malone, Ava would have sent her packing long ago. I don't know what's happening, but I suspect Deanna will get rid of the Brit in no time at all."

Unfortunately, she wouldn't have a chance to set Deanna straight because in a couple of days she would be back on a plane to the States, and on another one to England not long after that. She didn't have a reason to stay behind.

"Would you like a drink, Ms. Banks?"

She heard a sharp gasp and turned. The gasp had come from the gossiping women while the question was from someone who should have known better. The CIA operative named Drake stood in front of her, dressed in his server's uniform, a tray of drinks in his hand.

Even as she could hear the women moving away, she sent Drake a look to let him know she didn't appreciate the interference. But she could use a drink. "Yes, I'll take a martini. Gin. Up with a twist."

It looked like she would need it.

He frowned and tipped his tray her way. "But I have piña coladas."

"Then you're useless to me." She glanced back and JT was busy listening to an older man talk about the best golf courses. All three of their suspects were in the room, and it didn't look like they would be going anywhere. She could take a moment to check in with her team.

She strode toward the back of the large room to the big bar where Sandra Croft was mixing drinks. Luckily, everyone in the group seemed to be busy with their conversations. There were waiters winding through the party with drinks and appetizers, and no one was sitting at the bar. Sandra looked up from her blender and smiled Nina's way, sliding a martini glass in front of her.

They were alone with a good fifty feet between them and the party, so she hopped onto a barstool. "Thank god. I was worried I would have to drink those overly sweet things."

Sandra gave a prefilled container a nice shake and poured the drink over the twist of lemon that completed Nina's favorite cocktail. "I know what you like. I also know that you and the mister don't appear to be getting along."

"Yeah, I noticed that, too." Drake had followed her though he still had a tray full of piña coladas he'd been offering the guests. "I thought you were supposed to be engaged."

"And I thought you were supposed to be discreet," she shot back. "I was listening to that conversation." She looked to Sandra. "They were gossiping about my chances of surviving Deanna."

"Oh, I think they would be surprised at what you could do to that one." Sandra went to work pouring out some more drinks. "Though I think they're wrong about the assistant. I've been watching her all night. I don't think she's into JT. I think she's into her job, but not her boss. She doesn't look at him that way."

"There's a way to look at someone?" Nina asked.

"Yes," Sandra said with a chuckle. "It's this look of complete longing and desire. If you want to know what it looks like, I've got a mirror for you."

Nina rolled her eyes and took a long drink. "You've been talking to Taggart."

Drake frowned. "What is that supposed to mean?"

"Talking. Conversing. It's when two or more people exchange words," Sandra said. "In this case it was on a conference call. Hutch was there, too. That boy can eat. I thought he kept that candy on his desk because he wanted the kids to like him. I don't blame him. Tag's twins can be mean and bribery works with them, but he can pack away the sweets."

Drake raised a brow. "I was asking what you meant by Nina's got a look of longing. Because she better not be longing for the billionaire. Not in real life. Is that why you're not over there doing your job? You know they're all gossiping about why you and your fiancé have been so distant."

"She's been here for all of four hours," Sandra shot back. "Leave her alone. Do you know who isn't doing his job right now? It's you. People won't wonder why the new girl is sitting in the back talking to the bartender, but they might wonder why the new girl, the bartender, and some random waiter are having a meeting. Go, little boy. Serve drinks."

Drake's jaw tightened, but he picked up his tray. "I'm not joking, Blunt. Don't fuck this up with feelings."

Sandra shook her head. "He's a little asshole, but I'll get him in line in the end. Now tell Auntie Sandra what went wrong with the billionaire. Was he bad in bed? Because I wouldn't be surprised. That boy is so pretty he doesn't have to be good in bed. I'm working on that with Drake, too. Pretty boys need to try harder."

"He's incredible in bed," she replied before Sandra's words really sank in. "Wait. What? You're sleeping with the…" She lowered her voice. "You're sleeping with your young coworker?"

What she wasn't saying was *you're sleeping with the CIA guy who could turn out to be truly dangerous.* And also happened to be young enough to be her son.

Sandra shrugged. "There's actually not a lot to do here, and Hutch and I decided it would be an excellent way to keep track of him. One of us had to do it and Hutch was surprisingly whiny about his personal sexual preferences. So I took one for the team. Why? You want him? Because he's not great at oral yet."

She choked on her gin but managed to get it down. Working with Sandra was always full of surprises. "No. You should keep that going. It's obviously working since he's out peddling piña coladas and we've got a chance to talk. Is everything in place?"

"Of course it is," Sandra replied. "Hutch is watching us right now. He says hi and he wants to know why you broke it off with the hottie, too. He's in my ear, but he's also got eyes on us."

So Hutch had taken over the security system. She'd noted the multiple cameras that covered the resort. She'd also made sure their suite with one bloody bed was bug free. "How does Hutch feel about the rest of the staff?"

"He ran reports on everyone working at the resort. They're all solid, almost all local," Sandra said. "With the exception of a couple from the mainland, but they've all been here for six months or more. I feel comfortable the other side doesn't have any plants on staff. Now stop evading the question."

She should have known Sandra would be a bit like a hound who'd caught a scent. She wasn't about to let it go. "We have a difference of opinion. We ran into a spot of trouble, and we didn't agree on how to handle it. He tried to call off the mission."

"Ah, so shit got real and he got scared. I'm going to assume it was fear for you because he's a man and he doesn't understand that we can shoot guns, too."

"I don't think it's the shooting part that he minds, but he does seem to take exception to my getting shot," Nina explained. "Apparently he finds my job distressing."

Sandra's eyes rolled. "And he broke it off with you over that?"

He hadn't exactly broken things off. He'd tried to talk to her. It had been a lucky thing for her that they hadn't been alone on the private jet or she wasn't sure what would have happened since every time the man looked at her she threatened to melt. "No. He tried to stop the mission or leave me out of it. I broke it off with him."

"But you're here so you obviously won that fight. Why break it off with him? Unless he's a sore loser. I kind of thought you were into him."

"I was. I still am." Nina glanced back over her shoulder and he was nodding at something Jordy was saying. Deanna stood at his side, yawning as though she was bored as hell. "But he lied to me. He knew who I was and pretended not to because he knew I wouldn't sleep with him if I'd known we were going to work together."

"But you probably would have," Sandra pointed out.

"No, I wouldn't." She'd thought about this all night long. She'd sat up in her lonely bed and wondered if she would have been able to resist him if he'd decided to seduce her. Would she have turned down those lips on hers? Told him she didn't want those big hands on her body? Perhaps not, but the choice had been taken away from her and the choice was the whole point.

Sandra shifted and looked around her. "You sure about that because he's pretty hot."

She didn't need to go there. Deflection was her friend, and the truth was she needed to do her job. "Do we have any information on our pickup man?"

Sandra looked like she wanted to argue but she merely sighed and moved on. "We know he's on the island." She glanced to her right, nodding. "Aren't you supposed to be working?"

Greg Hutchins eased behind the bar. He was carrying a tool kit. He was not much older than Drake, but somehow he seemed more mature. There was a calmness about the man they called Hutch that she found soothing. "I need to move the camera over the bar. It's not getting the coverage I want. I thought I could bring our friend up to speed while I work. No one should question it since it's my actual job."

Sandra went to work on another batch of piña coladas. "Anything new?"

He went up on his toes and started playing around with the small camera that covered this section of the bar. "Yeah, he's definitely here on the island. Our spy came in on a fake passport. He flew from Seoul, but we think he was in North Korea last week. I got off the phone with Tag a few minutes ago and he's found some interesting tidbits in the world of banking. Looks like the assistant recently took out a five-thousand-dollar loan, and yet that money isn't in her account. She's either got a secret one we haven't found yet or she made a big purchase in cash."

"Or she hired someone for a job they don't want on the books." Like running them down the night before.

"That's what I was thinking," Hutch said. "But I also know the other two have some very complex monetary situations. They're both old money, and old business money at that. I'm going to have our forensic accountant take a look at it, but I think we're going to ID our suspect in person before we track them down financially. I'm taking the late shift the next couple of days and if I see anything, I'll give you a call. Sandra and I are in constant contact, and we can't seem to ditch the kid."

"Apparently Sandra's giving him lessons," she replied wryly.

Hutch frowned Sandra's way. "That was her choice. I tried to tell her I could plant some bugs he'll never find, but she chose to go this way. You know he's young enough to be your son."

Sandra rolled her eyes. "My daughter is way older than Drake. You have to get them young, Nina. You're right to dump that pretty boy. He's what? Thirty-two? You know what they say about old dogs. My little puppy there is learning lots of new tricks."

Drake set his tray down. "Tricks? What new..." He flushed. "Seriously? I didn't think we were going to talk about that. Like that's private."

"Not if I get you in a club it won't be. I think you'll like a little humiliation play." Sandra replenished his supply of fruity cocktails.

"I will not," he said in a way that made Nina think he might. He picked up his tray and turned. "People are talking, Ms. Blunt. And they're watching you."

Then it was time to go. She picked up her martini and turned, bumping into a mass of muscle.

"Hey, I think we're about to go in to dinner." JT loomed over her. "We should probably sit together."

"You should definitely sit together," Drake said under his breath before he stalked off.

"He's a handful, but look at that tight little ass," Sandra said with a sigh.

JT's eyes widened.

Nina found she couldn't hold out on him. She'd hated not talking to him all day. She'd gotten used to their friendship, to the easy way they seemed to fit together.

It was only a few more days. She could survive being close to him. She slid her arm through his. "Come on. Take me to dinner where your assistant will shoot daggers my way, and later on I'll tell you all about Sandra and her May-December romance."

"I'm not that old," Sandra groused. "May-October, maybe..."

"I'm going to need that story," JT said, his free hand coming up to cover hers. His voice went low. "But he's right. I do think people are talking about us. I think I've come up with a way to stop them."

"Holding hands should help."

"Or we could give them something else to talk about. I mean, that's kind of our job, right? I'm supposed to distract them so you don't seem threatening in any way, so they think you're only here because I couldn't stand the thought of leaving you behind." He'd stopped right at the edge of the crowd and she found herself being turned from his side until she was standing right in front of him, looking up into the greenest eyes she'd ever seen.

All day she'd managed to keep some distance between them, but she was now reminded of how much chemistry they had. Her body didn't care that he'd lied to her, that he'd tried to get her kicked off her own op. Her body only remembered what it felt like to be skin to skin with him.

His hands came up, cupping the sides of her face. "It's for the mission."

She found herself nodding. Yep. For the mission.

He lowered his head and his lips were on hers.

The whole world seemed to drop off, and all that mattered was the heat that flashed through her. His fingers wound in her hair and she felt surrounded by him. He turned the kiss deep and utterly carnal, his tongue surging into her mouth and coaxing hers to dance.

One of his hands moved down her back to her waist, pulling her in even closer so she could feel the hard planes of his chest against her breasts, crushing her deliciously to him.

He kissed her one last time and then whispered. "That should do it. I think if I kiss you like that a few more times, there won't be any doubt as to how much I want you, how much I am unwilling to give you up. For anything."

He moved to her side again, and there was a lazy smile on his face as Deanna stood staring at them, one hand on her hip.

"If you're done, we should go in to dinner," she said, her irritation plain.

"Oh, I'm not done. Not even close." He brought Nina's hand up to his lips. "But I'll behave for now."

His fingers tangled with hers and he started toward the dining room.

She suddenly had the unnerving feeling he wasn't talking about the mission at all.

She took a deep breath because if JT had decided to fight dirty, she wasn't sure she could win.

* * * *

It was all about sex. That was how he would get to her.

Dinner had flown by. He was sure it had all been delicious, but it hadn't mattered. It could have been undressed kale salad with a bit of dirt clinging to it for all he'd tasted the food. All he'd been able to think about was her, but then that was pretty much his whole life right now. Nina twenty-four hours a day, seven days a week.

He wasn't sure how he would get through the next few days without making a complete fool of himself since everyone could tell how crazy he was about her.

And everyone could easily see she wasn't that into him.

"I think dinner went well," Nina said, emerging from the smaller of the bathrooms. She'd taken it over before he could convince her to stay in the master bedroom.

"Did it?" He hadn't gotten ready for bed. He'd walked in, wanting to talk to her only to have her disappear, but that was what she'd been doing since the moment she'd found out about his lie.

She hadn't walked away because he'd acted like an ass about her job. She'd walked because he'd lied to her.

She'd brushed out her hair and taken off her makeup. She was gorgeous with makeup, and she was gorgeous without it. He was rapidly discovering he liked every single version of the woman in front of him. He wanted her whether she was wearing a sexy cocktail dress or the cotton pajama bottoms and tank top she had on now.

"I learned a little more about our suspects, though I don't think at this point it matters," Nina said, keeping a careful distance. "Hutch is staying up and he'll be monitoring the security feed. Sandra is monitoring Drake since they're worried the tech might disappear if we let him roam."

"Can't have free-range operatives," he murmured. He'd thought about this all day, thought about how to reach her. "I hated today."

She flushed, her skin going a sweet pink that let him know she wasn't cold even under her chilly exterior. "I'm sorry. It should be over soon. The North Korean operative is on the island. I'm fairly certain this won't take the whole week. Then we can be done."

That was what he wanted to avoid. "I didn't hate working with you. I hated not being close to you. I hated the fact that you're frowning and it's my fault."

"It's certainly not your fault."

"Nina, I lied to you. I thought it didn't mean anything at the time, and I'm going to be honest. I still don't fully understand why it hurt you so much, but I want to. I want to understand everything about you so I don't ever hurt you again."

She seemed to suddenly find the floor endlessly interesting. "You won't hurt me again."

"Because you won't give me another chance?" There seemed to only be silence between them. "I didn't say this before but I'm sorry. Whether or not you're willing to give me a chance, I am so sorry I hurt you. You're important to me. Your happiness is important to me and the fact that I was the cause of your unhappiness is killing me."

Her eyes came up, searching his. "Why?"

He would give her nothing but honesty from here on out. No matter how vulnerable it made him. "Because I'm pretty damn sure I'm falling in love with you. I think you're the one for me and I think I'll be lonely for the rest of my life if I'm not with you. It's funny. I was lonely for a long time after Mike went into the Navy. I was used to him being close. He was always there. Since the moment we were conceived, my brother was next to me. I hate the fact that I didn't see he needed so much more. I'm worried I'm making the same mistake with you."

"I wouldn't say I need more. I merely believe…I don't think this can work between us."

"Why?" he asked, desperate for the answer. "If you don't want me, I will back off. It will kill me, but I don't want to be that guy who tries to force his way into a woman's life. But if it's something else, I think we should talk about it."

She hesitated for a moment. "It's too much, too fast."

"What should it be? How much time do you need because I'll give it to you."

"I don't know. I don't know that we can go back," she admitted.

He couldn't let her go. Not without one last try. "But sometimes things happen fast. We can't shove them to the side because they didn't happen on some timetable."

"I'm going home to England when this job is done. I can't…I can't give up my career and let you pay for everything. It's funny because I literally read these books all the time where that's the happily ever after, but I've realized it's not for me." Before he could object, she held out a hand. She moved to the couch farthest from him and sank down. "I know you haven't asked me to do that, but I think that's what it will come down to. You'll want me to travel with you. You'll want me to host your dinners and do much of what I did tonight. I think I would lose myself in that kind of life."

He hated the hollowness in her tone. "Okay, so we take a step back. You go home to England and maybe we talk. We slow things down."

She stared at the glass doors that led to the balcony. "I don't think we can go back. Tonight proved that. When you kissed me, I forgot every reason I was angry with you. None of it mattered."

Frustration welled up inside him. "I don't see how that's a bad thing. I think it proves we can work."

"It proves that I can't think straight when I'm around you." She turned his way. "I don't know that I'll be able to stay away from you."

"I don't want you to." He moved to the sofa she was sitting on. "I'm not demanding that you stay here. I'm telling you I'm willing to take anything you give me. I'm willing to slow down and I'll force myself to only call you once a week."

"But I don't think I'll be able to leave if I give in."

That was exactly how he wanted it. He moved in closer to her, letting his hand move over hers. If he could just get her in his arms, maybe all her doubt would be eased. Maybe what he really needed to do was take control. "Nina, you have the choice, but I think you're stuck in an analysis loop. I think you want something that you can't ask for."

She looked down at the place where his hand covered hers, but she didn't move away. "I don't think I should ask for it at all. I think I should walk away, but I can't make myself do it."

He leaned in. "All you have to do is tell me no. Tell me to stop and I'll sleep on the couch tonight."

There was such longing in her eyes as she looked up at him. "This won't solve any of our problems."

He thought she was wrong about that. He believed if he could get her in bed, he could remind her of all the ways he could take care of her. It went past sex. He could make her feel loved and secure. He could show her that he would put her first.

It was a startling revelation that he'd finally found a relationship that came before his familial responsibilities, beyond the company he'd devoted his life to. If he pursued this thing with Nina, he might still have a passion for his job, but she would be first in his soul.

It should have scared him. In some ways it did. He'd lost a lot of people he'd loved, but he also knew that if he closed himself off, he would never have this warmth in his heart, never have this certainty that this woman made him feel complete in a way he never would if she walked away. He would always take this chance.

"Let's take one night at a time," he cajoled.

"I'm going to leave at the end of this job. I have to." But she'd turned and her whole body seemed to have softened as though she was giving in even as she said the words. "I have to."

He intended to show her she could be his and not lose herself. "Like I said, I'll take whatever you will give me."

"Liar. You'll take everything." Her hands came up and she drew his head down. "The question is will I let you."

His lips touched hers and he didn't care about anything but the feel of her in his arms. She was soft and sweet and she'd gone gloriously submissive.

They'd talked a lot about play, but he'd never spanked her. He kissed her long and deep, and then pulled back and hauled her over his knee.

A shudder went through her. "Yes. God, yes."

It had been a long, rough day, and she needed an excuse to let out all that tension.

He needed this, too. Needed it like he needed air to breathe.

He dragged the pajama pants down, exposing her round, perfect ass. He let his hand run over the globes, loving how soft her skin was, anticipating how pretty it would be when it had a nice sheen of pink. "I'm going to give you fifty. Will that be enough?"

"If it's not I'll beg you for more."

He would love to hear her beg, but he wouldn't deny her. "Your safe word is a simple no, but I won't make you say it. I'll give you what you need."

He placed his left hand on the small of her back and brought his right hand up and down in a short arc that sent a loud smack through the room, followed by the sweet sound of her moan as she held on to him.

"That's exactly what I need. Please, JT."

This was what they both needed. To be together. To connect in a unique way that spoke to them both. He let instinct lead him, counting in his head as he lovingly smacked her ass over and over. He was careful, peppering the smacks across her skin, trying not to miss a single inch.

He slowed as he approached fifty. His whole body was ready for sex, but he didn't want this to end. The minute they were done, she would go back to being wary. He needed to make this last so they had time together, time to change her mind.

He stroked the flesh he'd slapped, feeling the heat trapped in her skin as she sighed and rubbed her cheek against his leg.

He let his hand ease between her legs and found the warmth of arousal he'd hoped to find there. Her pussy was slick and ready. He stroked her there, drawing out even more arousal. The spanking had done its job. It had relaxed her and gotten her ready for sex, but he wasn't ready to stop playing yet. Her legs were still trapped in the pajama bottoms, but he could find what he needed.

He caressed his way over her pussy, parting the labia and massaging the silky skin there. He slipped a single finger inside, fucking her gently.

"Oh god," Nina said, her breath picking up again.

"I missed you last night. I missed you like crazy." He hadn't known he could miss someone when they were physically with him, but he'd felt every moment of the distance between them like they were miles.

"I missed you, too. I've gotten used to sleeping with you," she admitted.

He'd gotten used to waking up with his arms wound around her, her hair tickling his chest. She seemed to like to sleep with her head on his chest. He would wake up and just lie there until she stirred.

He continued to stroke inside her with his middle finger while he let the pad of his thumb find her clitoris. Like the rest of her pussy, it was ripe and ready, her spanking having prepped her for pleasure. Every soft moan that came from her let him know he was hitting all the right spots.

His cock pulsed, but he ignored it, concentrating everything he had on her. It would be his moment soon enough.

Her whole body stiffened and released as a fresh rush of arousal coated his fingers. She went limp over his lap.

He hated the thought of waking up without her, of spending a single day without her voice in his ear, her body in his arms.

She eased off his lap and managed to get to shaky feet. He worried for a moment that she would step away from him, but she merely kicked off the PJ pants and dragged the tank over her head, revealing the body he was crazy about. He took in her graceful curves and the way her nipples puckered.

"Tell me what you want from me," she said, her voice thick with some unnamed emotion.

Everything. He wanted her heart and soul, but she wasn't ready to give them to him, might never be ready for that. "You. Only you."

She shook her head. "Play with me, JT. It's all I can do now."

He heard the weariness in her voice and felt it in his soul. If that was all she could give him, then he would take it. "What do I want? I want you on your knees. I want my cock in your mouth. I want you to suck me until I tell you to stop and then I want you to ride me until I can't fuck you anymore."

He would worry about the rest tomorrow. Tonight he would let everything go. He would be with her. They had days on this island. He would be patient and win her over the same way he'd done it in the first place—by showing her how he felt, by binding her in pleasure and intimacy.

He stood up and had her in his arms in an instant, easily hauling her up.

Her arms went around his neck as he carried her to the bedroom. "No one's ever carried me before."

He would do it every day. Her feet didn't need to hit the floor.

"Except emergency services, but I don't think that should count," she said in a dreamy voice.

He did not need to hear that, but he wasn't letting fear rule him. Besides, everything Big Tag and Alex had said to him he'd taken to heart. "That doesn't count in any way."

"Well, the nice lads who took me to hospital certainly didn't do that first part," she said on a sigh. "And I didn't want to see either of them naked."

That was also a good thing. He set her on her feet and dragged his shirt over his head. Her hand came up and touched his chest. His breath caught at the feel of her hand on his skin. It trailed down his chest to the buckle of his belt.

She dropped to her knees in front of him. "Do you know how long I've wanted to get this cock in my mouth?"

He'd held her off because he'd wanted to give to her, but perhaps that had been a mistake. He sucked in a breath as she carefully unzipped his slacks and dragged them down his thighs. He'd taken off his shoes and socks when they'd gotten back to the room, so it was easy for her to toss his slacks aside.

Yes, it had been a mistake to not let her give to him. There was an eager look in her eyes that sparked his own need further. When she pulled down his boxers, his cock sprang free, hard and wanting everything she could offer him.

"Touch me." He growled out the command, satisfied with how she immediately obeyed, her hand reaching for his cock and gripping him. "Yes, that's exactly what I want. Stroke me."

She did as he requested, her eyes on him. Her hand moved up and down his cock. He was hard, but the feel of her soft skin grasping him made him even harder.

"Lick me."

Her lips curled up as though she knew that despite the fact she was on her knees, she was the one with all the power here. It was the beauty of the exchange. They both got what they needed. He got to pretend he had control and she got to understand exactly how much he wanted her. Needed her.

Her tongue came out and swiped across the head of his cock, sending heat flashing through his body. He watched as she sucked him between her lips lightly. It was a teasing caress. She settled back on her knees and drew him in again. His dick disappeared behind her lips, sinking into the silken heat of her mouth. She found a rhythm that threatened to send him over the edge. She pulled at him, giving him the barest scrape of her teeth. The tiny pain lit him up and he fisted her hair, gently guiding her on and off his cock.

He let her continue until the heat got to be far too much, until he could feel his balls draw up and prepare to shoot off. He wasn't doing that in her mouth. He wanted the hot clasp of her pussy.

He tugged on her hair and stepped back, grabbing the condoms he'd put in his bag in a burst of optimism. With shaking hands, he rolled one over his cock and then moved back to her, offering to help her up. The minute she was on her feet, he pulled her into his arms and set his lips on hers. He didn't play around. He immediately coaxed her mouth open and let his tongue surge in as he turned and moved her toward the bed.

They crashed down, their bodies molding together like they'd been made for each other. He felt the soft mattress as he settled against it.

He kissed her again and then let his head fall back. "I told you what I want. Don't make me spank you again."

Like that would happen. He wouldn't have the patience to start over, but he didn't want to stop the play.

She smiled like she knew what had just gone through his head. She kissed his jaw and then straightened up, straddling his hips. He could feel the heat of her pussy right where he needed it. "I believe you told me to ride you until you couldn't fuck me a second longer."

She rolled her hips and he hissed as pleasure swamped his every sense. She moved over him, rubbing against him and making him groan in a mix of frustration and bliss.

"Stop teasing me," he managed to growl. Maybe he could spank her. And then fuck her senseless.

She shifted and he was right where he wanted to be. She lowered herself onto his cock, inch by glorious inch.

He let his hands find her hips, helping to guide her up and down. He slammed up, thrusting deep inside her and watching her as she moved over him with sensual grace. She was the single sexiest woman he'd ever seen, and it was about so much more than her gorgeous face and body. There was a glow about her that drew him in again and again.

She shuddered above him and let out the sweetest moan.

It was his turn. He flipped her onto her back and took complete control. She wrapped those long legs around his waist as he slammed into her. It wasn't more than a few hard thrusts before he was careening over the edge, his whole body alive with pleasure.

He dropped down, letting her have his full weight. She merely wound her arms around him and held him tight.

They lay that way for the longest time, unwilling to break the connection.

# Chapter Ten

The buzz of her mobile brought her out of sleep long before she would have wanted. She was warm, her body sated and replete with the pleasure JT had lavished on her. After the first time, he'd slowed things down, but he hadn't let her sleep until she'd come four more times. There was a delicious ache in her backside that reminded her of how good that man was at giving a spanking.

She glanced at the clock. Almost two in the morning.

She wanted to stay in bed with him, their bodies wrapped around each other like they fit together even though she was terrified they didn't. In the dark she could pretend she never had to make a decision at all.

But the buzzing of that mobile reminded her she had a job to do. After all, only a few people had that number and not one of them would call at this hour if it wasn't important. She eased out of bed, the mobile in her hand, and made her way to the luxurious bathroom in an attempt to not wake her sleeping billionaire.

Would things be different if he was a normal guy? If he was normal, he might be willing to move to be closer to her rather than being forced to insist on the opposite.

She closed the door between them and looked down at the screen.

*Multiple suspects on the move. Sandra and the kid are tailing the boys, but the assistant is walking around the grounds acting sketchy as hell. I'm not sure if she's high or drunk or making her play. Should I leave my monitor and follow her?*

She quickly dialed his number. "Don't move. I need you to keep eyes on everyone. Have you seen the spy?"

"I haven't, but I suspect the drop is going to be somewhere I don't have cameras," Hutch explained. "I'm betting on the beach, since it would be easy to meet in the middle and they wouldn't need a car."

"Where is Deanna?" If Sandra and Drake were following the men, she could certainly take on JT's assistant.

"She's been pacing by the pool. She was on her phone for a while. When Jordy walked by, she hid."

So she didn't want anyone to see her. "Are Jordy and Patrick together?"

"They're both in the bar, but they're at different tables. Patrick is talking to another one of the guests, but he's been off and on his phone. Jordy's alone and he keeps looking at his watch," Hutch explained.

"He told JT he was heading to bed the last time we talked to him." He'd been one of the last people at the party, and she'd watched him walk out of the bar. Why had he gone back?

"Sandra and Drake have both exits covered and intend to follow them. I contacted you because I'm worried that the bar is about to close and we'll need a third set of eyes," Hutch relayed. "I'm in contact with our friends, but I'm concerned about the assistant. She's carrying what looks like a heavy bag. I don't think that was what she was using earlier."

Deanna had been carrying a clutch at dinner. It had barely been big enough to hold a mobile and some lipstick. "I'll shadow her. My room is fairly close to the pool. You stay where you can watch us, and let me know if anything else happens. Including with Drake."

She didn't want him to think he could waltz off with the prototype. She was certain JT would get it back at some point, but only after the US government had studied it and figured out a way to use it, thereby cutting Malone Oil out.

"Will do."

She hung up and reached for the clothes she'd folded earlier in case she needed to slip out. At least she'd prepared for one thing. The rest of the evening she hadn't thought once about the job. From the moment JT had put his hands on her, all she could think about was him.

She could get so lost in him. Like her mom had been in her dad right up until the moment he'd walked out on them.

God, was that what this was about? Not Roger, but her dad? JT was nothing like her handsome, ne're-do-well father. JT was almost slavishly devoted to his family in a way her father had never been. Even as a youngster she'd known her father wasn't good for her mother.

And JT wasn't good for her concentration. She quickly dressed and checked her gun, easing it into the shoulder holster she covered with a light sweater, and then she was sneaking out.

She caught a glimpse of JT in the moonlight, his cut chest on full display. He was so gorgeous, so giving. Losing him would kill her. When she'd found out about Roger's betrayal, she'd thought her heart had been broken. She couldn't even imagine what it would be like to lose JT. Her heart wouldn't merely break. It would shatter into a million pieces, and there would be no putting it back together.

She shook off the thought and strode to the outer room, picking up the small earpiece she'd placed on the bar and settling it in. She touched it.

"Sandra, can you hear me?"

"Loud and clear." Sandra's voice was in her ear.

Nina brushed her fingers through her hair, hiding the earpiece in case she ran into anyone. She'd seen a couple of vending machines near the pool. She could fake that she'd gotten lost looking for them. "Do you have eyes on Jordy?"

"I have eyes on everyone I need to have eyes on," Sandra replied. "He's getting fidgety. Jordy, that is. Drake is proving to be perfectly patient. He's outside, and from what I can see, he hasn't moved a muscle. He's good at blending into the background. Patrick has no idea he's being watched."

That was a skill that would help the kid enormously at the Agency. "I'm going to try to do the same with Deanna. Let me know if anything changes."

"Will do."

Nina pocketed her room key and slipped outside. The hallway was quiet at this time of night, though it was brightly lit. It reminded her of how she was used to working in the shadows.

She strode down the hall and moved into the stairwell. The lift would be easier, but it was also more unpredictable. She'd taken a tour of the grounds when they'd gotten in so she could familiarize herself with the place. The pool was at the eastern end of the building. It was a huge space, with a large infinity pool overlooking the ocean.

She jogged down the four flights of stairs and slipped outside, the sounds and scents of the ocean seeming to take over all her senses. Without the music that played in the pool area during the day and long into the night, the sound of waves crashing against the beach became the night's soundtrack. Warm wind caressed her skin and she once again wished she was here for the normal reasons. If she was simply here to relax with her boyfriend, this would be one of the most romantic spots in the world, with the moon shining down and the air soft around them.

But a voice in her ear reminded her that she wasn't here for any of those reasons.

"Jordy is on the move," Sandra said in her ear, her voice barely audible, which made her think she was being super cautious. "He started for the path that leads to the beach, but he saw me. I fucked up. He turned and walked the other way."

"Patrick is finishing up his last drink, and it looks like he's going to try to get laid," Drake said. "I think he's a bust. I'll try to see if I can follow Jordy. Sandra, switch with me and make sure Patrick goes back to the hotel."

"I'm moving into position," Sandra replied.

"Drake, if you take the path to your left, you'll move in behind Jordy." Hutch's voice was perfectly calm, though Nina knew they were moving into a danger zone.

Chaos was the enemy.

She strode quietly down the path that led to the largest of the pools. She stopped at the edge of the patio, keeping behind the big bushes that surrounded the space, giving it an illusion of privacy. Deanna was pacing, staring down at her phone as though it was some kind of a lifeline. She had a big beach bag on her shoulder, and she'd changed from her cocktail dress to black jeans and a T-shirt, trainers on her feet and her hair in a ponytail.

She looked like she was ready to run if she needed to. In the short time she'd known Deanna, the woman had always been dressed in a completely professional way, even in a casual setting.

Then again, she also hadn't seen Deanna looking anything but confident, and that was not how she looked now. She put the phone to her ear.

"Jay? Yeah, I'm going to do it." She was quiet for a moment. "I know. I know. I don't care. He owes me and I'm going to collect. After this, there won't be any way I don't get what I want. I'm done playing by his rules." She went silent again. "I don't care what he thinks about it. He can fire me. I'm done waiting. Like I said, if this doesn't work, nothing will."

Shite. She moved back and touched her earpiece. "I think I've got our traitor. It's Deanna."

"I haven't been able to dupe her phone yet," Hutch admitted. "So I don't know who she's talking to, but she's moving. She just hung up and she's walking your way. Nina, she's going to see you."

Nina moved in between two high bushes. They were covered in fragrant flowers and provided adequate concealment. And scratches to her arms, but it wasn't anything she couldn't handle. She pushed her body further back and went completely still.

"I'll be careful," Deanna was saying as she walked by. "It's okay. I've got a gun. I'll use it if I need to."

And now she had to deal with an armed Deanna.

"Nina, you're in the clear," Hutch said. "But she's not going where I thought she would. She's moving back toward the main building. Stay out of sight. I've got her on camera."

Nina moved out of the bushes and back onto the path, adrenaline starting to thrum through her system. This was going down here and now. They had apparently been wrong about the beach, though.

"Hey, my guy is about to get into a cab," Drake said.

"No problem," Hutch replied. "I rented a motorcycle. Sandra's got a key and it's in the parking spot right off the main lot. The cab will have to stop at the main gate to the resort. I'm in control of that gate. I'll keep you close. You okay following him on your own?"

"I can be there in two minutes," Sandra replied. "Patrick has his tongue down this chick's throat. I think it's safe to say he's going to her room for the night."

Nina didn't like the idea of letting one of their suspects go, but she also didn't like Drake being out on the island without backup. The only thing worse than him betraying the team would be getting himself killed. "Sandra, go with him."

She didn't like the feeling in the pit of her gut. Something was going on here and she was missing it.

"I'll keep eyes on Patrick," Hutch assured her. "Nina, Deanna's going into the hotel and she's heading for the elevator. Her room's in the other wing, so we know she's not going there. There's only one elevator working right now. You'll have to take the stairs."

She slipped through the door to the building and immediately into the stairwell. "I'm going to level three. Tell me when she gets out of the lift."

She jogged up the stairs, wanting to be somewhere in the middle.

"Hey, Nina, give me a second. I've got the cab coming through for

Jordy. I need to make sure they don't leave too quickly. Sandra is almost to Drake."

"I'm good here," she replied.

She took a deep breath and waited. The lifts had been slow earlier in the day. Even if Hutch missed Deanna getting out of the lift in real time, there were enough cameras covering the halls that he would be able to tell where she was going.

It was going to be all right. If Deanna disappeared into a room, they would stake the room out.

She would because Sandra and Drake would be following their other suspect. Did she want to split them up like this? Hutch would come running if she needed him to, but it could take him valuable minutes. Hutch seemed to think the spy wasn't on property, but there were any number of ways for a smart operative to sneak in.

She had to make sure they couldn't sneak out again.

She waited, every muscle in her body tense.

Maybe she was getting too old for this because a nice desk job seemed perfect right now. No one would wake her up in the middle of the night and drag her out of a warm bed so she could stand in a creepy stairwell waiting to see if someone would start shooting at her.

What was she going to do about JT? Was she really going to walk away? She couldn't stay, and she wasn't sure some weird long-distance thing had any shot of working.

What was taking Hutch so long?

"Nina, we have a big problem. Two, actually. Someone's piggybacking my feed from the outside. It's a pro because I should have caught it hours ago. That's how good this job was. I wouldn't have caught it if I hadn't needed the computer to deal with the gate. Someone else is watching." Hutch sounded breathless.

Fuck. It had to be the spy. "You said we had two problems."

"Deanna went to the fourth floor. She's got JT."

Nina's heart threatened to stop and she began to run.

\* \* \* \*

JT felt the moment Nina left the bed, but he remained perfectly still, determined to not blow this again. He knew there was only one reason she would leave the room and that was to work. Her cell had buzzed. Someone on her team wanted to talk.

She didn't need him trying to play the white knight. She was a professional and he would let her do the job.

Still, as he heard the door close his stomach was in knots. He slid out of bed and jumped into the shower. He wouldn't sleep until she came back.

Helpless. He felt completely helpless, but it was also the first time he'd had to lie here and pretend like she wasn't going to do something dangerous. Maybe he was looking at this the wrong way. So much of life was about adjustment, and he hadn't had time to adapt. He just had to get through about a hundred nights of praying no one shot the woman he loved and then he would be used to it.

He turned off the shower and grabbed a towel. He would never get used to it, but maybe he would be better about hiding how worried he was. He would find a way to put her at ease.

For now, he would make a pot of coffee and sit up waiting for her.

She might be mad, but he wasn't going back to bed. They would have to find a compromise because he couldn't let her go.

He pulled on a pair of sweatpants and a T-shirt and thought seriously about going down to the gym. He had a key. Maybe he could run his worry off.

But he quickly discarded the idea because she would want to talk to him if something had gone down tonight. He was the client in this case, and he might have decisions to make.

About people he'd known for years. He made his way to the coffeemaker and started a pot. It was still nauseating to think someone so high up in his organization could betray the company like this.

Deanna would be the worst. They weren't friends. They didn't hang out, but he had relied on her for years. He'd made sure she was the highest paid assistant in the business.

Although he couldn't help but think about what she'd said when he'd hired her.

*I'm not going to be an assistant forever, Mr. Malone. You will promote me and I'll be running part of this company in five years.*

That had been seven years ago.

Was she doing this because he'd passed her over for a promotion? When the position had come up, the timing couldn't have been worse. There had been some chaos in his office and he couldn't let her go. He'd promised her she would get the next job.

Was she tired of waiting? Had she found another way to get

everything she wanted?

It was hard for him to believe, but he had to consider it.

There was a knock on the door and he hurried to open it because it was likely Nina. She'd probably forgotten her key in her need to rush out. He swung it open and then realized he was a dumbass.

"JT, I'm sorry to wake you up so late, but we need to talk." Deanna was standing in the hallway.

A chill went over him. Had he been a fool all this time? Why the hell would she turn up at his door at two thirty in the morning? "Talk about what?"

She swung her head back and forth, looking down the hallway. "Can I come in? It's important. There's something going on that we need to talk about."

Fuck. Nina was going to kill him but he wasn't sure what he could do since Deanna strode right in, brushing past him in her normal brusque manner.

"What do we need to talk about?" He closed the door behind her but not before flipping the security latch out so the door wouldn't lock. He didn't want Nina to have to use her key. She would see the door was open and know something was wrong. She would be on her guard.

She set her bag down on the table near the bar. "First of all, you're an asshole. Second, where's your girlfriend?"

He put his hands on his hips and faced her. He wasn't about to tell her the truth—that he had no idea where Nina was but he kind of hoped she was riding in to the rescue right now. "She's asleep and she's not my girlfriend. She's my fiancée."

Deanna's eyes rolled. "We'll see about that. We all know how good you are at keeping your word when it comes to promotions."

So she *was* pissed. Was that the reason she'd decided to betray him? Was she about to offer him a deal? His mind was racing. How should he handle this? Should he go along with her until Nina came back? He could play this role if he had to. The key was to not let her see him sweat. "What's going on, Dee?"

"How much do you really know about her?" Deanna's face had gone stony.

"Enough. If this is about trying to get rid of my fiancée, you should leave." He was going to feel like the biggest idiot in the world if he'd worked with her all this time and never seen that she was crazy about him. He knew he wasn't the world's most self-aware human being, but he should have seen this coming. She hated every woman he went out with. He'd written it off because she hated a lot of people, but now he had to consider the fact that he'd been wrong. "Deanna, you have to know nothing is going to happen between us."

Her eyes widened. "What?"

That should be his question. What was she playing at? And why was she pulling this stunt now? "I know you set a private investigator on her. You're not going to find anything that makes me turn from her to you. I don't have those feelings for you, Dee. I'm sorry. This is never going to happen."

"This?" Deanna's face had gone a bright pink, but he wasn't sure it was embarrassment. It looked more like rage, but then lots of emotions looked like rage on her. "This meaning a relationship between you and me that I am supposedly desperate for because no woman in the world could possibly not want you?"

Definitely rage, and he might have been mistaken. "Now, Dee, maybe you should…" Nope. He wasn't saying *calm down*. Calm down was bad. Saying the words *calm down* never actually calmed any woman down. "Talk about this some more. I might be under a mistaken impression."

"Mistaken? About what exactly? Were you confused because I did my freaking job? Do you honestly believe I've worked my ass off out of love for you? Because I thought you would one day look at me and realize I'm the love of your life? You're confused because I was fucking good at my job and that must mean I'm desperate for some man, any man. Because that's obviously the only reason a woman would ever do her job."

"Well, you did spend a whole lot of this week trying to get me away from Nina." He wasn't completely insane. She'd done a lot to try to come between them.

"Yes, you moron, because I think she might be dangerous," Deanna bit out. She shoved her hand into her bag. "I can't believe you haven't seen what the hell was going on around work, but then you don't see anything, do you, JT? As long as your calls are answered and someone's doing all the inane work so you can climb oil rigs, you really don't care."

He was starting to get annoyed. "I never meant to take you for granted. You've been an excellent assistant, despite the fact that you don't mind insulting the hell out of the boss apparently."

"And you think I'm insulting you because I'm upset you won't ever love me? You think I want to get rid of Nina so I can take her place? Well, then you'll probably misinterpret why I brought this along." She pulled her hand out of the large bag.

And JT took a step back because that was one big-ass gun in her hand. "Hey, now…"

She frowned his way. "Chill your balls. I'm not planning on using it on you."

Oh, god, had she come for Nina? Was she going to kill Nina right in front of him? He started to think about how to get that gun out of her hand. "Nina's not here."

Deanna's eyes rolled and she let out a frustrated groan. "I don't think Nina is who you think she is, JT. Something is going on. Something you missed. I don't think Bill's accident was really an accident."

He went still. "You know what happened to Bill?"

Deanna might have said something, but the door burst open and Nina moved in with the fluid grace of a predator. He heard the door smack against the latch again, leaving it slightly open.

"Put the gun down," she said tightly. "JT, get behind me."

He moved to her side. But he couldn't get behind her. He knew if he had to, he would stand between her and a bullet because he wouldn't be able to live with himself if he didn't.

Deanna held her gun up and looked like she knew exactly what she was doing. It shouldn't surprise him. Deanna was always determined to be an expert at anything she did. "JT, Nina is not who she says she is. Why the hell do you think I set a PI on her? Do you think I like spending money? He's not cheap." She stared Nina's way. "I know exactly who you are. You're here to make money off him. You're not only a gold digger, you're a criminal."

Nina's jaw went tight. "And you're sad. You're in love with a man who doesn't want you. Put down the gun."

Deanna's eyes narrowed. "I do not want JT. I couldn't care less about the man, but I do want the fucking job I was promised, and apparently I have to do it all. I have to be the most organized human being on the face of the planet, smile while I'm being marginalized by every man in the room, and now I have to hunt down corporate spies. If you're looking for your friend, Nina, tell him I took back our prototype and he can pry it out of my cold, dead hands."

She'd done what? He was about to ask the question when there was a pinging sound, and he watched in horror as Deanna slumped to the floor.

Patrick stood in the doorway. His plan to give Nina a heads-up had worked against them and allowed the snake into the room.

Nina turned and slammed into JT right before the gun went off again. Patrick fired wildly, trying to take them out. JT dropped to the floor and his head smacked into the side of the couch so hard he would have sworn he could see stars.

"Deanna, you stupid bitch," Patrick said with a snarl. "That will teach you not to steal from me. Sorry, JT. I didn't mean to kill anyone, but a man does what he must."

# Chapter Eleven

Nina shoved herself up and cursed under her breath as she tried to tuck JT closer to the base of the couch. "Don't move."

She wasn't sure where Patrick was and she'd completely lost control of the situation. Hutch had said something about Patrick in her ear as she'd rushed into the room, but she hadn't paid attention to him. All she'd been able to think about was JT and getting to him in time to save him from Deanna.

It turned out Deanna had been trying to save him from her. Apparently the assistant had figured out something was wrong and had decided to fix it all herself.

Now she was likely dead, and if Nina didn't calm the fuck down and think like an operative and not a crazy scared girlfriend, they would be dead, too.

"I want that prototype," Patrick was saying.

She had to stall him long enough to either take a good shot or give time for Hutch to get here. In her panic to get JT out of the line of fire, her earpiece had dislodged so she had no way of knowing how far away he was.

"So the fiancée is really a bodyguard." Patrick sounded like he was moving into the room. The suite was huge, and he would have to move past the sofa they were using as cover if he wanted to get to the table where Deanna's bag lay.

She glanced down at JT.

He winced but gave her a nod that let her know he was all right.

"I guess that means you knew something was wrong," Patrick continued.

She shifted to a crouch and realized there was a mirror over the bar. She could see Patrick standing warily at the edge of the room, as though he hadn't decided if he was going to go for the prize or run away.

"Keep him talking," Nina whispered.

"You couldn't think we wouldn't realize the prototype was gone," JT said.

"I was hoping you would think Bill had hidden it somewhere. I thought I would have a little more time," Patrick replied. "Where is it? Deanna obviously stole it out of my room earlier tonight. I've got a meeting in thirty minutes and I don't like to think about what will happen if I don't make it to the beach."

Probably the same thing that happened to Bill. But at least she knew where and when the drop was supposed to be. All she had to do was survive and she could catch the spy.

"I don't know where it is." JT moved so his back was to the couch. He watched in the mirror, too, as Patrick started to inch his way toward Deanna's body. "She hadn't gotten to the part where she told me what was going on. I thought she was upset I was engaged."

A nasty chuckle came from Patrick. "Yes, we've all thought she was pathetic, hanging around when it was obvious you weren't ever going to fuck her. Or promote her."

Nina kept her eye on the mirror. She could feel JT behind her. She wished there was some way to get him out of this, but he needed to stay down. If he moved for the bedroom, he would be exposed, and she didn't trust that Patrick wouldn't shoot anything that moved. She studied him carefully and his arm was already shaking. He wasn't used to holding a gun for so long. She would bet he'd had minimal training at best. It was dangerous since he wouldn't know how to control himself or the weapon he held.

There it was again—that horrible anxiety that something could happen to JT and she would spend the rest of her life mourning him.

"If you don't know where the prototype is, I don't have a lot of use for you," Patrick said, though there was a tremor in his tone.

"How do you think you're going to get out of this?" JT's voice was strong and steady. "Nina works for a private security company, but she's got ties to the government. Yeah, that's right. They know something's happening, and they won't stop looking for you even if you do manage to kill me. So the question is do you want to add another murder to what's going to be a long time in prison for you?"

Nina's heart was thumping in her chest, adrenaline flowing through her system. She could see the way this would play out in her head. Two more steps from Patrick and she could ease around the side of the couch, pop up, and plant two squarely in his chest.

Two more steps and it would all be over.

Patrick stopped. "If I kill the two of you it can look like a lover's quarrel. I can make it look like Nina found out about you and Deanna and killed you both then herself. That's what women do when they lose their shit."

Where the hell was Hutch? Patrick wasn't moving. He seemed stuck in a loop, trying to figure a way out of a trap that wasn't ever going to let him go. The longer she waited, the more chance he would figure it out and come to the conclusion that nothing mattered. A desperate man was a dangerous man.

"Or you could take the prototype in Deanna's bag and run," JT offered. "I think it's probably in her bag. She came up here to tell me about what she'd learned. Dee is smart. She knew something was going on and she tried to solve this thing herself. She came close. She figured out it was you."

"Nosy bitch never could stay out of things that didn't involve her," Patrick said, but he started moving toward the table again.

One more step.

Patrick came into clear view and Nina stood, took her aim, and fired. And again, taking out both lungs.

She watched his eyes flare and he put a hand to his chest. His gun clattered to the floor and then he followed.

She took a deep breath, banishing her panic. It was over. At least this part. She looked down at JT. "You can come out now. He's dead."

JT got to his feet, his skin sheet white. "Are you okay?"

Nina nodded. "I'm fine, but I have to make a couple of calls."

"I really do think the prototype is in her bag," he said. "She stole it earlier and she was bringing it to me. Damn. I can't believe he shot Deanna. I need to see if she's all right."

He started to move toward where his assistant lay, but nearly jumped out of his skin when her seemingly dead body sat up.

Deanna looked around, a wild look in her eyes. "Where's my gun?"

Nina moved to her and noticed there wasn't a drop of blood on Deanna's T-shirt, though it sported a nice hole in the chest. She held a hand out. "Body armor?"

Deanna took it and let Nina haul her up. "Of course. What? You think I would walk into some criminal shit without protection? My dad was a cop. And I am always prepared." She winced. "Though I wasn't prepared for how much that would hurt."

"You're all right?" JT stood back as though he wasn't exactly sure what to do.

She wanted to wrap her arms around him, but the job wasn't over yet.

Deanna looked down at Patrick's body and pointed. "Am I all right? No, I am not fucking all right. You gave this asshole my promotion. Mine. You want to go find Jordy now that Patrick's gone and hand the job to him? He's out looking for drugs, you know."

JT shook his head. "Nope, it's all yours. As of right now you are the VP in charge of operations."

Deanna glared his way. "I want ten percent more than what this asshole was making. And I want the company to pay me the five grand I spent on PIs and all the crap I needed to do this job."

"Done," JT said.

"And a budget to redo the office because his is nasty." Deanna brought her foot back and kicked the dead body. "Try shooting me again, moron. That was my fucking job."

The cops would love processing this scene. Not that they would actually ever get to the scene. The Agency would have a cleaning crew here in no time.

The door came open and Nina brought her gun up only to breathe a sigh of relief as Hutch walked through.

His eyes widened as he took in the body on the floor and the petite blonde who was kicking and cursing at it.

"Don't mind her," Nina said, striding over to the table and opening the bag there. "She's over-stimulated. It's been a rough night. Ah, here's what we've been looking for."

She pulled out the small prototype. Such a tiny thing to have caused so much trouble, but then technology came in all sizes.

"I'm sorry," Hutch said, sliding his gun back into his holster. "When I realized Patrick had used the woman in the bar as a distraction, I started making my way here. But he wasn't content to let her go. He'd knocked her out in the stairwell. I had to make sure she was breathing. Are you all okay?"

She glanced over and JT was watching her warily. It was obvious he wanted to talk.

But she still had a job to do and she wasn't sure what they should talk about. It was almost time to leave.

Almost time to leave him.

Could she leave him? She wasn't sure how she could possibly stay.

And she was doing it again. She was letting her feelings stop her from doing her damn job. "No problem, but you need to call Sandra and Drake back. I know where and when to catch our spy. We have to hurry."

"They're already on their way." Hutch slid a glance JT's way and then back to Nina. "I can handle this if you need some time."

She shook her head. Time was the one thing she didn't have. "No. Come on. We need to get down to the beach before our spy does or we'll lose him. JT, I need you to lock yourself in. I don't think anyone else is coming, but I can't be one hundred percent sure. I'll send Sandra up when she gets here."

Deanna had her gun in hand again. "I'll handle whatever happens. He caught me off guard. I'm actually really good with this thing."

"Nina," JT began.

She took the prototype and started for the door. "Not now. Stay here. I need to get down to the beach and find the spy."

"Or you could tell me where to go," Hutch started. "He'll be looking for someone like Patrick. I'm far closer in build. I think he'll run if he sees a slender female walking his way. I put on a hoodie and he won't be able to tell the difference." He touched his earpiece. "Sandra and Drake are on their way up to the hotel. They're already on property. They can back me up."

He wanted to shove her out of the op? "This is my mission."

"But it doesn't make sense for you to go," JT argued.

She ignored him. Somehow the idea of staying here and having it out with JT scared her more than standing in front of a spy who would be far better at killing than Patrick.

JT would ask her to stay, to give them a real chance. She would explain that her life was in London and she couldn't give up her whole career because she'd fallen madly in love with some man.

Except she didn't have to give it up. She could transfer to Dallas. Ian would let her do that. She knew there were a couple of people on the Dallas team who wanted to live in London for a while.

It could work.

It would be so stupid to change her whole life for a relationship that likely wouldn't last a year.

There was a knock on the door. "Hey, it's Drake. Let me in."

Hutch moved to open the door and the CIA agent walked in. "That was fast."

"Sandra's going to take over in the camera room. She's not as good with tech as you are," Drake said. "What happened here?"

"Patrick was our guy on the inside," Hutch explained.

"Patrick was a massive ass," Deanna added.

"We've still got a shot at picking up the North Korean spy." She was going to finish this job if it killed her. "According to Patrick, they're meeting on the beach like we thought. He's supposed to make the drop in about twenty minutes."

Drake nodded. "Excellent. Let's get moving. I'll call in a cleanup crew after we're done there. Civilians, try not to get too messy. It might be best if you went to another room until we're done."

Deanna looked up at JT. "We can use mine. I have a lot of changes I want to make. We can start talking about them while we wait for someone to clean up all the blood that got spilled because you picked him over me."

JT ignored her, moving to Nina's side. "I know you have to work and I'm not going to cause trouble, but promise me you'll come back to the room. I need to talk to you."

Yes, there it was. He was going to ask her to stay, to choose. She wasn't ready. Not even close.

"I don't think that's a good idea," she said under her breath.

He moved in closer. "Nina, I love you. Please give me a chance."

"Is that the prize?" Drake asked.

She slid her gun into the holster and placed the prototype on the table. "Someone should stay and guard it. I don't want the chance that our spy gets what he was after."

She started for the door.

"Holy shit." Hutch's jaw dropped. "When did JT get hit? Where is all that blood coming from?"

JT shook his head. "I'm fine."

Nina's breath caught because now she could see a dark stain starting to creep around the back of his shirt. Blood.

He'd been hit in that first wild volley of Patrick's and she hadn't even noticed. She'd shoved him down and then turned away from him.

JT's face went blank. "Why is my back wet?"

All thoughts of the job fled as JT hit his knees and the light began to fade from his eyes.

* * * *

JT blinked at the bright light that greeted him as he woke from the nicest dream. Nina had been at his side and there had been no questions in her eyes. Only love. Only joy.

She'd forgiven him. She'd loved him.

For a moment he clung to the dream, wanting to stay there, but then the pain hit and he remembered.

"Hey, brother," a soft voice said. "You doing all right?"

He forced his eyes open. Michael was standing over him and everything around him was stark and white.

Hospital.

"What happened?" It was fuzzy. One minute he'd been standing there in the suite at the resort. He'd been trying to tell Nina that he would wait for her, but she'd been so cold.

Then he'd realized that pain in his back had been more than a bruise from hitting the ground so hard.

"You were shot," a second voice said. His cousin, Simon, stood next to Michael. "You're in hospital. You took a bullet to the back. Unfortunately with all the moving about, the bullet shifted and came fairly close to one of your kidneys."

Michael grinned. "Don't worry. You've still got both of them. I was pleased since I'm the one who usually gets shot at and I take comfort knowing you're around to be my organ donor." He sobered slightly. "Mom flew down with us. Dad insisted on coming, too. They're having some lunch now."

He glanced around the small room. There was no sign of Nina. No purse left on a chair or blanket where she might have sat up next to his bed.

Had she simply left because the job was done?

"Did they finish the job?" It had been important to her.

"Yeah, they got it done," Michael replied. "We've filled in all the blanks. Patrick needed cash and badly. We managed to unlock his phone. It was all there. He hired someone to run you off the road when he found out it was you and not your dad going to the retreat. He still went through with it, though, because he needed the money. And the prototype is safely on its way to Dallas. Deanna flew back with it this morning. Hutch and Sandra escorted her, and they're going to make sure it's in the safe at the main office until you decide what to do with it. The new security liaison insisted on getting it to Dallas right away."

"Good." Nina was probably on her way back to London. She hadn't hung around very long. "Did they catch the spy?"

"Oh, yes." Simon was wearing one of his suits. Even in the tropics, his cousin wore a three-piece suit and managed to not get the damn thing wrinkled. "The Agency operative proved quite wily. He captured the spy and managed to not piss off Tag by trying to swipe the tech. The spy is likely being interrogated, and Drake isn't on the shit list. Given who's pulling the strings at the Agency these days, that's a miracle. Hutch was specifically here to ensure Drake didn't run off with the prize and present it to his boss."

He didn't know what any of that meant. His brother had gone on and on about someone named Levi and all the shit he'd stirred, but it didn't matter.

"So we figured out that Dee went to Houston and lied about it because she was investigating Bill," Michael explained. "She was surprisingly forthcoming in her debrief. And she knows a lot of ways to call a man a moron."

"My wife was impressed with her," Si agreed. "Apparently she'd caught some odd expenses on the engineer's reports and decided to investigate. She also said she told you but you weren't interested."

"Bill always had odd expenses." He should have listened to her.

"You okay?" Michael was looking at him with concern he hadn't seen in years. "I can get the doc in here if you need pain meds. You've been in and out, but they're going to start to wean you off. I can tell them to wait on that if you need the drugs."

If he took more, he might be able to dream about her again.

Or he could get healthy and go after her. He could stop being a whiny baby and prove to her that he was worth her time.

He shook his head. "No. I want to be clearheaded. How soon can I go home?"

He would go home but not for long. Just long enough to get his shit together and put in for a few months' leave. Then he would find a place in London and put his whole life on hold while he pursued the most important part of it. Her.

"A couple of days." Michael looked over at Simon. "Maybe we

should go tell them he's awake. I don't think they'll want to miss it if he goes back to sleep."

"No." He knew his parents would be worried, but he had to ask the question. "Give me a minute. I need to ask you something and I need to make sure you're going to tell me the truth."

"Nothing hit your dick, man," Michael quipped. "According to the docs it's still fully functional."

Simon rolled his eyes. "Ask me, JT."

"Did she even stay around to see if I was okay?" He wasn't sure it would matter. If she'd left then it had been because she was scared. He'd lied to her and put her in a corner, and she was afraid she would cease to exist if she stayed with him, that she would lose something essential about herself in the face of being his wife. He would show her that she was wrong.

Simon frowned. "Are you asking about Nina?"

Michael's expression had lost its humor. "She's gone, but I don't think it's for long."

"She's coming back? To Dallas?" She might have work to do there.

"No," Simon corrected. "She's coming back to the room. She's barely left it, but your mother insisted she eat a proper lunch."

Nina was here? "She's okay? She didn't get hurt tracking down the spy?"

"JT, she wasn't involved in that," Simon replied. "She hasn't left your side except when you were in surgery. She's been worried sick. Though she did manage to talk Michael out of a job."

"She can deal with Dad now." Michael breathed a sigh of relief. "I've been trying to convince Big Tag to let someone else be the liaison with Malone Oil for years."

The door swung open and sunshine walked in. Nina was wearing a T-shirt and jeans and she looked weary, as though she hadn't slept in days.

She was the single most gorgeous thing he'd ever seen.

She stopped and tears filled her eyes. "You're awake."

He was alive because she was here with him. He held a hand out. "Baby, please come close. I need to see you."

She rushed to him, taking his hand in hers. "How are you feeling? Are you in pain? I can talk to the doctors. Your mum and dad are with them right now because we want to fly you back home. They're making arrangements."

He brought her hand to his chest. "I'm fine and I'll go anywhere as long as you're with me."

"Wow, Tag is right," Michael said. "This does kind of make me gag."

Nina shot his brother a look that could have frozen fire. "Then you should leave because I'm about to tell your brother that I love him and I'm staying in Dallas and dating him until we've reached an acceptable time to become truly engaged. I will then marry him and we will proceed to have a few children, grow old and enjoy our lives together. And he's not going to lie to me ever again."

Now he was the one having trouble with tears. His eyes had gone watery. "Never. But, baby, you have to know I wouldn't take it back because I want everything you just promised me."

She leaned over and brushed her lips against his. "Then tell me you love me."

That was the easiest command he'd ever followed. "I love you."

"I'm going to find Mom and Dad." Michael put a hand on his stomach. "I can't take much more of that."

Simon shook his head but started to follow him out. "Only because you've never had it, cos. One day. One day."

But this was his day. His day to find forever. He drew her close and promised to never let her go.

# Epilogue

*Six months later*

JT looked around the elegantly decorated space with a deep sense of satisfaction.

This time it was for real.

"Happy engagement," his brother said, giving him a hearty slap on the back. "Nina looks stunning tonight. She's far too good for you."

He glanced over where his fiancée was laughing at something Chelsea Weston was saying. Chelsea grinned as she held her ten-month-old daughter. Sophy Weston looked an awful lot like her father.

"Mom dotes on that kid," Michael said with a sigh.

His mother treated Sophy like her grandchild, and constantly hinted that she would like some more. Nina was on board, but they were going to enjoy being a couple for a little bit before starting their family. Nina liked a schedule. They'd stuck to her original plans. She'd moved to Dallas and they'd dated for five months. Then he'd taken her on a trip to London to see her family and friends and asked her to marry him and she'd finally gotten to wear that gorgeous Tiffany ring for real.

He could still remember the glow in her eyes when she'd said yes. It was how he would always see her, vibrant and beautiful, nodding her head because words had failed her.

"Well, it's a good thing since Si's parents are in England and Chelsea's are gone," he pointed out. "I know Sophy has plenty of family around, but there's nothing like a doting grandmother. Dad's crazy about her, too. They're going to ride us both hard until we present them with an appropriate number of kiddos for them to spoil."

Michael shook his head. "That's all going to be on you, brother."

"Right now it is," he replied. "But one day you're going to join me."

"I don't think that's going to happen for me. Not the way it has with you and Nina," Michael replied with grim certainty. "I've never once been in love. I think you got all those genes."

"That's bullshit. You've had plenty of girlfriends over the years."

"And I never once looked at any of them the way you do Nina. I've never felt the need to chase after a woman the way Si did Chelsea," his brother pointed out. "I've never felt that, and I don't think I ever will. You and Si are lucky, you know."

Nina looked his way and winked at him before welcoming Charlotte Taggart into their little group.

He was the luckiest man in the world. But his brother was wrong. "You haven't met the right person yet. You should let Mom set you up."

His brother's face went the tiniest bit green. "Don't you even start that."

Simon strode up, a glass of Scotch in his hands. "Start what?"

"My brother here has decided since he's now getting married that it's my turn," Michael said with a frown.

Simon nodded Michael's way. "Well, you're not getting any younger. We've just hired a few new investigators. One of them is a lovely young woman. She's funny and quite bright. I can arrange a meeting."

Michael started to back away. "What is wrong with you people? I can find my own dates. I do not need a walking, talking version of Tinder. What happened?"

"Marriage. Children," Simon said with a shrug.

"Yep, I'm going to avoid all those things," Michael declared. "I'm going to be everyone's Uncle Mike. Now if you don't mind, I'm going to go drink a whole lot of beer and pretend you two haven't lost your damn minds."

He practically ran away.

"That's one way to scare my brother off," JT said with a shake of his head.

"He'll be back." Simon looked out over the party. "I think I'll arrange that meeting anyway. Lola is lovely, and she understands the constraints of his job. I think that's what's gone wrong with his last few girlfriends. He needs someone in the business."

He loved working with Nina. It was the perfect arrangement because they weren't together all the time, but when he traveled, she could go with him as his security expert.

His super sexy bodyguard.

"I think Mike will work it all out in the end." He smiled because Nina was walking his way. "Our ladies are here."

Chelsea and Sophy were by Nina's side, and Simon set down his drink so he could take his daughter. The baby girl grinned up at her dad.

That would be him someday.

Nina moved to his side, watching his cousin's family with a warm glow that let him know she was thinking the same thing.

She slipped her hand into his. "Are you ready? Your mother wants to make the formal announcement. Though I don't understand why. Everyone knows we're engaged."

"My aunt is extremely proud to have you in our family," Simon explained. "She never thought JT would get married. You should be ready for all the formalities. She's got a proper English girl in the family now."

Chelsea nodded. "Yeah, Aunt Ava has spent way too much time surrounded by dudes. I for one am super happy to have another woman around. Come on, my loves. Let's go find Mommy some champagne."

"Congratulations, you two," Simon said as he joined his wife.

JT turned to the woman who'd made his life brighter than it had ever been. He'd had a charmed life, but Nina made it a worthwhile life. He drew her close. "You ready to make it official?"

She tilted her head back and gave him a gorgeous grin. "Absolutely."

He leaned over and kissed his soon-to-be bride. With his friends and family all around him, life was finally perfect.

\* \* \* \*

Also from 1001 Dark Nights and Lexi Blake, discover Enchanted, Protected, Close Cover, Arranged, Dungeon Games, Adored, and Devoted.

Sign up for the 1001 Dark Nights Newsletter
and be entered to win a Tiffany Key necklace.

There's a contest every month!

Go to www.1001DarkNights.com to subscribe.

**As a bonus, all subscribers can download
FIVE FREE exclusive books!**

# Discover 1001 Dark Nights Collection Seven

THE BISHOP by Skye Warren
A Tanglewood Novella

TAKEN WITH YOU by Carrie Ann Ryan
A Fractured Connections Novella

DRAGON LOST by Donna Grant
A Dark Kings Novella

SEXY LOVE by Carly Phillips
A Sexy Series Novella

PROVOKE by Rachel Van Dyken
A Seaside Pictures Novella

RAFE by Sawyer Bennett
An Arizona Vengeance Novella

THE NAUGHTY PRINCESS by Claire Contreras
A Sexy Royals Novella

THE GRAVEYARD SHIFT by Darynda Jones
A Charley Davidson Novella

CHARMED by Lexi Blake
A Masters and Mercenaries Novella

SACRIFICE OF DARKNESS by Alexandra Ivy
A Guardians of Eternity Novella

THE QUEEN by Jen Armentrout
A Wicked Novella

BEGIN AGAIN by Jennifer Probst
A Stay Novella

VIXEN by Rebecca Zanetti
A Dark Protectors/Rebels Novella

SLASH by Laurelin Paige
A Slay Series Novella

THE DEAD HEAT OF SUMMER by Heather Graham
A Krewe of Hunters Novella

WILD FIRE by Kristen Ashley
A Chaos Novella

MORE THAN PROTECT YOU by Shayla Black
A More Than Words Novella

LOVE SONG by Kylie Scott
A Stage Dive Novella

CHERISH ME by J. Kenner
A Stark Ever After Novella

SHINE WITH ME by Kristen Proby
A With Me in Seattle Novella

*And new from Blue Box Press:*

TEASE ME by J. Kenner
A Stark International Novel

FROM BLOOD AND ASH by Jennifer L. Armentrout
A Blood and Ash Novel

QUEEN MOVE by Kennedy Ryan

THE HOUSE OF LONG AGO by Steve Berry and MJ Rose
A Cassiopeia Vitt Adventure

THE BUTTERFLY ROOM by Lucinda Riley

# Discover More Lexi Blake

### *Enchanted*: A Masters and Mercenaries Novella by Lexi Blake

*A snarky submissive princess*

Sarah Steven's life is pretty sweet. By day, she's a dedicated trauma nurse and by night, a fun-loving club sub. She adores her job, has a group of friends who have her back, and is a member of the hottest club in Dallas. So why does it all feel hollow? Could it be because she fell for her dream man and can't forgive him for walking away from her? Nope. She's not going there again. No matter how much she wants to.

*A prince of the silver screen*

Jared Johns might be one of the most popular actors in Hollywood, but he lost more than a fan when he walked away from Sarah. He lost the only woman he's ever loved. He's been trying to get her back, but she won't return his calls. A trip to Dallas to visit his brother might be exactly what he needs to jump-start his quest to claim the woman who holds his heart.

*A masquerade to remember*

For Charlotte Taggart's birthday, Sanctum becomes a fantasyland of kinky fun and games. Every unattached sub gets a new Dom for the festivities. The twist? The Doms must conceal their identities until the stroke of midnight at the end of the party. It's exactly what Sarah needs to forget the fact that Jared is pursuing her. She can't give in to him, and the mysterious Master D is making her rethink her position when it comes to signing a contract. Jared knows he was born to play this role, dashing suitor by day and dirty Dom at night.

When the masks come off, will she be able to forgive the man who loves her, or will she leave him forever?

\* \* \* \*

*Protected*: **A Masters and Mercenaries Novella by Lexi Blake**

A second chance at first love

Years before, Wade Rycroft fell in love with Geneva Harris, the smartest girl in his class. The rodeo star and the shy academic made for an odd pair but their chemistry was undeniable. They made plans to get married after high school but when Genny left him standing in the rain, he joined the Army and vowed to leave that life behind. Genny married the town's golden boy, and Wade knew that he couldn't go home again.

Could become the promise of a lifetime

Fifteen years later, Wade returns to his Texas hometown for his brother's wedding and walks into a storm of scandal. Genny's marriage has dissolved and the town has turned against her. But when someone tries to kill his old love, Wade can't refuse to help her. In his years after the Army, he's found his place in the world. His job at McKay-Taggart keeps him happy and busy but something is missing. When he takes the job watching over Genny, he realizes what it is.

As danger presses in, Wade must decide if he can forgive past sins or let the woman of his dreams walk into a nightmare…

\* \* \* \*

*Close Cover*: **A Masters and Mercenaries Novel by Lexi Blake**

Remy Guidry doesn't do relationships. He tried the marriage thing once, back in Louisiana, and learned the hard way that all he really needs in life is a cold beer, some good friends, and the occasional hookup. His job as a bodyguard with McKay-Taggart gives him purpose and lovely perks, like access to Sanctum. The last thing he needs in his life is a woman with stars in her eyes and babies in her future.

Lisa Daley's life is going in the right direction. She has graduated from college after years of putting herself through school. She's got a new job at an accounting firm and she's finished her Sanctum training. Finally on her own and having fun, her life seems pretty perfect. Except she's lonely and the one man she wants won't give her a second look.

There is one other little glitch. Apparently, her new firm is really a front for the mob and now they want her dead. Assassins can really ruin a fun girls' night out. Suddenly strapped to the very same six-foot-five-inch hunk of a bodyguard who makes her heart pound, Lisa can't decide if this situation is a blessing or a curse.

As the mob closes in, Remy takes his tempting new charge back to the safest place he knows—his home in the bayou. Surrounded by his past, he can't help wondering if Lisa is his future. To answer that question, he just has to keep her alive.

\* \* \* \*

### *Arranged: A Masters and Mercenaries Novella* by **Lexi Blake**

Kash Kamdar is the king of a peaceful but powerful island nation. As Loa Mali's sovereign, he is always in control, the final authority. Until his mother uses an ancient law to force her son into marriage. His prospective queen is a buttoned-up intellectual, nothing like Kash's usual party girl. Still, from the moment of their forced engagement, he can't stop thinking about her.

Dayita Samar comes from one of Loa Mali's most respected families. The Oxford-educated scientist has dedicated her life to her country's future. But under her staid and calm exterior, Day hides a few sexy secrets of her own. She is willing to marry her king, but also agrees that they can circumvent the law. Just because they're married doesn't mean they have to change their lives. It certainly doesn't mean they have to fall in love.

After one wild weekend in Dallas, Kash discovers his bride-to-be is more than she seems. Engulfed in a changing world, Kash finds exciting new possibilities for himself. Could Day help him find respite from the crushing responsibility he's carried all his life? This fairy tale could have a happy ending, if only they can escape Kash's past…

\* \* \* \*

### *Dungeon Games: A Masters and Mercenaries Novella* by Lexi Blake

Obsessed

Derek Brighton has become one of Dallas's finest detectives through a combination of discipline and obsession. Once he has a target in his sights, nothing can stop him. When he isn't solving homicides, he applies the same intensity to his playtime at Sanctum, a secretive BDSM club. Unfortunately, no amount of beautiful submissives can fill the hole that one woman left in his heart.

Unhinged

Karina Mills has a reputation for being reckless, and her clients appreciate her results. As a private investigator, she pursues her cases with nothing holding her back. In her personal life, Karina yearns for something different. Playing at Sanctum has been a safe way to find peace, but the one Dom who could truly master her heart is out of reach.

Enflamed

On the hunt for a killer, Derek enters a shadowy underworld only to find the woman he aches for is working the same case. Karina is searching for a missing girl and won't stop until she finds her. To get close to their prime suspect, they need to pose as a couple. But as their operation goes under the covers, unlikely partners become passionate lovers while the killer prepares to strike.

\* \* \* \*

### *Adored: A Masters and Mercenaries Novella* by Lexi Blake

A man who gave up on love

Mitch Bradford is an intimidating man. In his professional life, he has a reputation for demolishing his opponents in the courtroom. At the exclusive BDSM club Sanctum, he prefers disciplining pretty submissives with no strings attached. In his line of work, there's no time for a healthy relationship. After a few failed attempts, he knows he's not good for any woman—especially not his best friend's sister.

*A woman who always gets what she wants*

Laurel Daley knows what she wants, and her sights are set on Mitch. He's smart and sexy, and it doesn't matter that he's a few years older and has a couple of bitter ex-wives. Watching him in action at work and at play, she knows he just needs a little polish to make some woman the perfect lover. She intends to be that woman, but first she has to show him how good it could be.

*A killer lurking in the shadows*

When an unexpected turn of events throws the two together, Mitch and Laurel are confronted with the perfect opportunity to explore their mutual desire. Night after night of being close breaks down Mitch's defenses. The more he sees of Laurel, the more he knows he wants her. Unfortunately, someone else has their eyes on Laurel and they have murder in mind.

\* \* \* \*

### *Devoted: A Masters and Mercenaries Novella* by **Lexi Blake**

*A woman's work*

Amy Slaten has devoted her life to Slaten Industries. After ousting her corrupt father and taking over the CEO role, she thought she could relax and enjoy taking her company to the next level. But an old business rivalry rears its ugly head. The only thing that can possibly take her mind off business is the training class at Sanctum…and her training partner, the gorgeous and funny Flynn Adler. If she can just manage to best her mysterious business rival, life might be perfect.

*A man's commitment*

Flynn Adler never thought he would fall for the enemy. Business is war, or so his father always claimed. He was raised to be ruthless when it came to the family company, and now he's raising his brother to one day work with him. The first order of business? The hostile takeover of Slaten Industries. It's a stressful job so when his brother offers him a spot in Sanctum's training program, Flynn jumps at the chance.

*A lifetime of devotion….*

When Flynn realizes the woman he's falling for is none other than the CEO of the firm he needs to take down, he has to make a choice. Does he take care of the woman he's falling in love with or the business he's worked a lifetime to build? And when Amy finally understands the man she's come to trust is none other than the enemy, will she walk away from him or fight for the love she's come to depend on?

# No Love Lost

Masters and Mercenaries: The Forgotten, Book 5
By Lexi Blake
Coming September 29, 2020

When Ezra Fain joined the ranks of the CIA, the last thing on his mind was romance. After meeting Kim Soloman, it was difficult to think of anything else. A tragic mistake drove them apart, leaving him shattered and unable to forgive the woman he loved. But when his greatest enemy threatens her life, Ezra leaps into action, prepared to do anything to try to save her.

Solo accepted long ago that she won't get over Ezra. She's worked for years to get back into his life, looking for any way to reignite the love they once shared. Unfortunately, nothing seems to penetrate the wall he has built between them. When she's arrested for a crime she didn't commit, she believes she's on her own.

Racing across the globe, Ezra and Solo find themselves together again, caught in the crosshairs of the agency they sacrificed so much to serve. Days on the run soon turn to steamy nights, but Levi Green isn't about to let them find their happily ever after. And when the smoke clears, the men and women of McKay-Taggart will never be the same again.

# About Lexi Blake

*New York Times* bestselling author Lexi Blake lives in North Texas with her husband and three kids. Since starting her publishing journey in 2010, she's sold over three million copies of her books. She began writing at a young age, concentrating on plays and journalism. It wasn't until she started writing romance that she found success. She likes to find humor in the strangest places and believes in happy endings. She also writes contemporary western ménage under the name Sophie Oak.

Connect with Lexi online:

Facebook: www.facebook.com/lexi.blake.39
Website: www.LexiBlake.net
Instagram: www.instagram.com/Lexi4714
Twitter: twitter.com/authorlexiblake
Pinterest: www.pinterest.com/lexiblake39/

# Discover 1001 Dark Nights

HIDDEN INK by Carrie Ann Ryan
BLOOD ON THE BAYOU by Heather Graham
SEARCHING FOR MINE by Jennifer Probst
DANCE OF DESIRE by Christopher Rice
ROUGH RHYTHM by Tessa Bailey
DEVOTED by Lexi Blake
Z by Larissa Ione
FALLING UNDER YOU by Laurelin Paige
EASY FOR KEEPS by Kristen Proby
UNCHAINED by Elisabeth Naughton
HARD TO SERVE by Laura Kaye
DRAGON FEVER by Donna Grant
KAYDEN/SIMON by Alexandra Ivy/Laura Wright
STRUNG UP by Lorelei James
MIDNIGHT UNTAMED by Lara Adrian
TRICKED by Rebecca Zanetti
DIRTY WICKED by Shayla Black
THE ONLY ONE by Lauren Blakely
SWEET SURRENDER by Liliana Hart

COLLECTION FOUR
ROCK CHICK REAWAKENING by Kristen Ashley
ADORING INK by Carrie Ann Ryan
SWEET RIVALRY by K. Bromberg
SHADE'S LADY by Joanna Wylde
RAZR by Larissa Ione
ARRANGED by Lexi Blake
TANGLED by Rebecca Zanetti
HOLD ME by J. Kenner
SOMEHOW, SOME WAY by Jennifer Probst
TOO CLOSE TO CALL by Tessa Bailey
HUNTED by Elisabeth Naughton
EYES ON YOU by Laura Kaye
BLADE by Alexandra Ivy/Laura Wright
DRAGON BURN by Donna Grant
TRIPPED OUT by Lorelei James
STUD FINDER by Lauren Blakely
MIDNIGHT UNLEASHED by Lara Adrian
HALLOW BE THE HAUNT by Heather Graham

DIRTY FILTHY FIX by Laurelin Paige
THE BED MATE by Kendall Ryan
NIGHT GAMES by CD Reiss
NO RESERVATIONS by Kristen Proby
DAWN OF SURRENDER by Liliana Hart

COLLECTION FIVE
BLAZE ERUPTING by Rebecca Zanetti
ROUGH RIDE by Kristen Ashley
HAWKYN by Larissa Ione
RIDE DIRTY by Laura Kaye
ROME'S CHANCE by Joanna Wylde
THE MARRIAGE ARRANGEMENT by Jennifer Probst
SURRENDER by Elisabeth Naughton
INKED NIGHTS by Carrie Ann Ryan
ENVY by Rachel Van Dyken
PROTECTED by Lexi Blake
THE PRINCE by Jennifer L. Armentrout
PLEASE ME by J. Kenner
WOUND TIGHT by Lorelei James
STRONG by Kylie Scott
DRAGON NIGHT by Donna Grant
TEMPTING BROOKE by Kristen Proby
HAUNTED BE THE HOLIDAYS by Heather Graham
CONTROL by K. Bromberg
HUNKY HEARTBREAKER by Kendall Ryan
THE DARKEST CAPTIVE by Gena Showalter

COLLECTION SIX
DRAGON CLAIMED by Donna Grant
ASHES TO INK by Carrie Ann Ryan
ENSNARED by Elisabeth Naughton
EVERMORE by Corinne Michaels
VENGEANCE by Rebecca Zanetti
ELI'S TRIUMPH by Joanna Wylde
CIPHER by Larissa Ione
RESCUING MACIE by Susan Stoker
ENCHANTED by Lexi Blake
TAKE THE BRIDE by Carly Phillips

INDULGE ME by J. Kenner
THE KING by Jennifer L. Armentrout
QUIET MAN by Kristen Ashley
ABANDON by Rachel Van Dyken
THE OPEN DOOR by Laurelin Paige
CLOSER by Kylie Scott
SOMETHING JUST LIKE THIS by Jennifer Probst
BLOOD NIGHT by Heather Graham
TWIST OF FATE by Jill Shalvis
MORE THAN PLEASURE YOU by Shayla Black
WONDER WITH ME by Kristen Proby
THE DARKEST ASSASSIN by Gena Showalter

*Discover Blue Box Press*

TAME ME by J. Kenner
TEMPT ME by J. Kenner
DAMIEN by J. Kenner
TEASE ME by J. Kenner
REAPER by Larissa Ione
THE SURRENDER GATE by Christopher Rice
SERVICING THE TARGET by Cherise Sinclair
THE LAKE OF LEARNING by Steve Berry and MJ Rose
THE MUSEUM OF MYSTERIES by Steve Berry and MJ Rose

## On Behalf of 1001 Dark Nights,

Liz Berry, M.J. Rose, and Jillian Stein would like to thank ~

Steve Berry
Doug Scofield
Benjamin Stein
Kim Guidroz
Social Butterfly PR
Asha Hossain
Chris Graham
Chelle Olson
Kasi Alexander
Jessica Johns
Dylan Stockton
Richard Blake
and Simon Lipskar

Made in United States
North Haven, CT
29 September 2024

58092018R00118